Warwickshire & The West Midlands
Edited by Lynsey Hawkins

Disclaimer

Young Writers has maintained every effort
to publish stories that will not cause offence.

Any stories, events or activities relating to individuals
should be read as fictional pieces and not construed
as real-life character portrayal.

First published in Great Britain in 2006 by:
Young Writers
Remus House
Coltsfoot Drive
Peterborough
PE2 9JX
Telephone: 01733 890066
Website: www.youngwriters.co.uk

All Rights Reserved

© Copyright Contributors 2006

SB ISBN 1 84602 686 5

Foreword

All children love to read and be read to, and what would delight a child more than writing their very own piece that others can read and have read to them?

Young Writers was established in 1991 to promote the written word amongst school children. Now, in 2006, we are still encouraging children to put themselves forward and to challenge their own talents, especially through specifically tailored projects such as our short story challenge promoted through primary schools nationwide.

To ensure the writer was challenged and that the books offer a variety of writing styles and themes we offered pupils the opportunity to write a short story on a theme of their choice. Alternatively they could have used one of the following to inspire their piece; *the ini Saga*, a story of 50 words or less; the saga has a beginning, middle and end, often with a twist in the tale. *Nursery Rhymes Fairy Tales* - we suggested the idea of pupils writing a letter to a character such as Fantasy Forest Council writing to the Big Bad Wolf. As well as that inspiration could be drawn from the theme to write a monologue, a spell, to re-tell a fairy tale, change the ending or even mix and match the characters in stories!

Each piece was chosen on the basis of style, technical skill, ability to entertain and flair for writing, and from the many entries we received, we have produced an outstanding 'Small Talk' series of books, with the pieces written by 7-11 year-olds, all illustrating how imaginative today's children can be. *Small Talk Warwickshire The West idlands* is our latest offering which we are sure you will agree is a fantastic collection, not only showcasing the pupils' work, but the school's ability to inspire and let the children's creativity flow.

We hope you continue to enjoy this delightful collection again and again for it is truly inspired and a credit to all who are featured within the following pages.

Contents

Dawley Brook Primary School, Kingswinford
Anna Davies (9)	1
Scott Coley-Smith (9)	2
Jade Barnes	3
Beth Newey (9)	4
Tom Hanlon (9)	5
Alex Marson (9)	6
Calum Johnson (9)	7
Tom Willets (9)	8
Paige Moberley	9
Matthew Anson	10
Kirby Timmins (10)	11
Philippa Grove	12
Emily Bennett	13
Aidan Griffin	14
Liam Snape	15
Emma Taylor (9)	16
Jared Whapples (9)	17
Selina Garner (9)	18
Anna Morris	19
Kay Bennett	20

Fallings Park Primary School, Wolverhampton
Ryan Pickin (9)	21
Phillip Garner (10)	22
Macaulay Love (10)	23
Georgina Jefimik (11)	24
Jessie Ansell (9)	26

Ferncumbe CE Primary School, Warwick
Naomi Cruden (10)	27
William Dews (10)	28
Charlie Hanson (11)	30
Simon Wyatt (10)	31
Charlotte May (10)	32
Joe Edwards (11)	33
Connor Ball (10)	34
Callum Adams (10)	35

Manor Way Primary School, Halesowen
Rosie Poliquin-Hill (9)	36
Emily Rose Hill (9)	37
Christian Herbert (9)	38
Laura Nicholson (9)	39
Matthew Bateman (8)	40

Oaklands Primary School, Birmingham
Laura Chui (9)	41
Aqeela Zafar (10)	42
Tia Brown (10)	43
Faith Scanlon (10)	44

Our Lady of Lourdes Primary School, Birmingham
Helen Mockler (10)	45
Alessandro Barwani-Rai (10)	46
Lubna Amir (10)	47
Conor Burns (10)	48
Natalie Rahill (10)	49
Zoe Tubb (10)	50
Katie Rosina Warren (10)	51
Jade Amanda Crosbee (10)	52
Laura Patricia Horton (10)	53
Christine Cartlidge (10)	54
Ciarán McCarthy (10)	55
Regan Rowley (10)	56
Emily Treacy (10)	57

Palfrey Junior School, Walsall
Nagina Kauser (10)	58
Mitchell Pettifor (10)	59
Muhammad Patas (9)	60
Faiz Ahamad (8)	61
Mahfuja Akthar (9)	62
Shahed Miah (9)	63
Hamima (9)	64
Haleema Lorgat	65
Moaaza Nadat	66
Annie Marie Grainger (10)	67

Nazeerah Zainab Akbar (9)	68
Papiya Begum (10)	70
Mohammed Kasujee (11)	71
Zakirah Kalang (10)	72
Asiya Tahar (10)	73
Rahena Begum (10)	74
Ahmed Ali Tarajia	75
Sonia Waheed (10)	76
Juleka Begum (9)	77
Tayabah Kanwel (10)	78
Jumanah Kasujee (8)	79
Humaira Chowdhury (10)	80
Naeema Goni (10)	81
Waqar Syed (10)	82
Halima Begum	83
Tahmina Ahmed (9)	84
Rahima Begum Malik (10)	85
Sharmin Khatun (10)	86
Marriyah Hussain (10)	87
Nafisah Khatoon (10)	88
Akif Ahmed (10)	89

St Andrew's School, Birmingham

Sumaya Tuki (8)	90
Noha Said	91
Isha Sikander (8)	92

St Joseph's RC Junior School, Nuneaton

Joshua Claridge (9)	93
Haley Webb (9)	94
Harry Bennett (9)	95
Lily Lee (9)	96
Stephen Snounou (9)	97
Liam Hutchinson (9)	98
Olivia McAlinden (8)	99
Jacob Goddard (9)	100
Elle Simpson (9)	101
Marina Davidson (8)	102
Franklin Davies (7)	103

St Mary's Immaculate Catholic Primary School, Warwick
Curtis Simmonds (9) 104
Zoe Bench (11) 105
Anoosha Babu (11) 106
Ross Chamberlain (10) 107
Dannielle Hover (10) 108
Samuel Slemensek (10) 109
Yasmin Feasey (9) 110
Luke Smith (10) 111
Alexander Pilkington (10) 112
Blake Wareing (10) 113

Somerville Primary School, Birmingham
Khalid Saeed (11) 114
Suhail Chaudhry (11) 115
Sonia Khanum (11) 116
Shweb Uddin (9) 117
Zakia Kalsoom (9) 118
Kanwal Hassan (9) 119
Umair Badshah (9) 120
Sabera Begum (9) 121
Wasim Mehmood (9) 122
Irfhan Khan (9) 123
Zainab Jabeen (9) 124
Yasar Javed (9) 125
Zakia Amer (9) 126
Ariba Afzal (9) 127
Nosheba Shafiq (10) 128
Alina Choudry (9) 129
Salina Mahmood (9) 130
Khalida Begum (10) 131
Aisha Mohammoud (10) 132
Nabila Irshad (10) 133
Fozia Gul (10) 134
Madihah Hasan (8) 135
Amel Mohammed (8) 136
Jansheer Khan (8) 137
Danyal Hassan (9) 138
Shahid Zaman (9) 139

The Croft Preparatory School, Stratford-upon-Avon
Jenny Yule (8) 140
Savanaugh Robertson (8) 141
Henry Tribe (8) 142
Molly Wright (8) 143
Hugh Symons (8) 144
Anastasia Hall (8) 145
Molly Hughes (8) 146
Oliver Thomas (8) 147
Harriet Edwards (8) 148

St Joseph's RC Junior School, Nuneaton
Theresa Day (8) & Annie Bath (7) 149
Elissa Johnston (8) 150
Nadia Ahmed (8) 151

The Creative Writing

Cackle Cackle Ha Ha

This is what to do to send Cinderella to goo!
Let's chop my warts,
Get my hair,
Pull my teeth out
And we're ready to go
Catch that frog,
Squeeze, squeeze, squeeze
Er nasty
Cackle cackle ha ha
Very good job done by me!

Eyeballs
Frogspawn
Frogs' legs
Frog, frog, frog!
Hairy potatoes I was having for my tea!
Smelly ham,
Mouldy chicken,
Whack some bread in!
Stir, stir, stir,
Er er er
Cackle cackle cackle ha-ha, hee-hee
A very good job done by … me!

Anna Davies (9)
Dawley Brook Primary School, Kingswinford

The Shahethlik Spell

To make the prince slowly rot,
I will put all my ingredients into this pot,
Eyeballs and frogs' legs, with earwax as well,
It's easy to kill the prince with this evil spell,
Rats' tails and human blood,
Armpit hairs and snot,
Snapped off toenails, slimy dragon scales,
Now his rule will stop,
Rabbits' ears, hairy legs,
Foxes' poo and flesh,
Rotten bones and magic stones today is the prince's death,
Pour it onto a dinner plate,
I've tricked the prince like a piece of cake,
He will die at exactly 12 o'clock,
Now his rule will slowly stop.

Scott Coley-Smith (9)
Dawley Brook Primary School, Kingswinford

Dear Council

128 Swamp Land
Wonderland
Disney Paracel
USA

Dear Council,

I am writing to explain about Lord Farquahar because he keeps dumping all the fairy-tale creatures in my swamp and I do not like it!

They keep sleeping in my bed and eating all my food, it is ridiculous. Oh yes! And they keep having races, it is a nuisance. Please do something about it.

Yours sincerely,
Shrek.

Jade Barnes
Dawley Brook Primary School, Kingswinford

Witch's Spell

Eyeballs and frogs
A giant smelly foot,
Smelly earwax and a rat's pointy tail,
Blood from a boy,
Smelly old socks, a human's spit,
A little girl's ear, a bird's old eyes,
To kill Snow White for ever and ever,
Put her in a pot of frogs' blood and bats so
I can be pretty forever.
Ha! Ha! Ha!

Beth Newey (9)
Dawley Brook Primary School, Kingswinford

The Witch's Spell!

Hello Goldilocks, I am the witch of the north. Mmm ... I wonder what I'll do to you? Ahh! I know, I'll put some lava in a bin and put you in there until you're thin and put some slugs in to make your feet go in and out, and of course I'll know that you will be knocked out.

Troubles, troubles, lots of bubbles,
Troubles, troubles lots of bubbles.

I'll put some fire in your sack that makes your skin go black and black.

Ha, ha, ha, ha, ha, ha
Goodbye.

Tom Hanlon (9)
Dawley Brook Primary School, Kingswinford

The Forbidden Spell

First put in a vicious bird who cannot fly,
Mix it up with a dead dog's eye,
Then put a three-headed cerebus in
And smelly garbage from the bin,
Put a bit of sluggish bones,
Then put dead faces which moan and groan,
Wait for a while then throw in some slippery quails,
Let's hope this spell does not fail!
Put some goo on, nice and thick,
Finish it off with a bowl of sick!
All of this will rot their skin,
So now all three pigs will be bony and thin!

Alex Marson (9)
Dawley Brook Primary School, Kingswinford

The Smelly Pig's Spell

Rotten toast and mice,
A frog's leg with spice,
That would do quite nice.

A bear's toe and a bat's nose,
Dog's paw and a wart that shows,
That's a spell only me knows.

I, the Smelly Little Pig,
Will go down the path of the wolf,
To make him more nasty,
Where nobody goes!
Ha, ha, ha!

Calum Johnson (9)
Dawley Brook Primary School, Kingswinford

Dear Wolf's Parents

                                48 Magic Forest Lanes
                                Running Water House
                                Sweat Midlands

Dear Wolf's Parents,
   Your son, the Big Bad Wolf, has been blowing down our houses all week and I want a stop put to this right now. Please tell your son this because we haven't had any sleep in a whole week because we have to keep rebuilding out houses. If you don't we will build all of our houses out of bricks!
   Yours sincerely,
   The Three Little Pigs.

Tom Willets (9)
Dawley Brook Primary School, Kingswinford

Dear Council

45 Forest Road,
The Wood
DY7 592

Monday 26th June

Dear Council,

I am writing to complain about Goldilocks. She has broken into my house because my locks are broken! Even worse than that, Goldilocks has eaten our porridge and broken my baby's chair. If that wasn't enough she slept in our beds. Goldilocks is getting on my last nerve. I would like to say that I want Goldilocks to stay 55 feet away from me and my house.

Yours faithfully,
Papa Bear
Momma Bear
And Baby Bear.

PS: Can you fix my locks? Thank you.

Paige Moberley
Dawley Brook Primary School, Kingswinford

Dear Mr Holt

569 Forest Lane
Stream Park
Woodland
K72 4JB

Dear Mr Holt,

I am complaining about the three Billy Goats Gruff, who keep on trotting over my bridge. I've put signs and posters up to warn the goats. There is also another bridge but the goats go on mine. Can you help me to find a way for the goats not to trot over my bridge? Let me know as soon as possible.

Yours faithfully,
Mr Troll.

Matthew Anson
Dawley Brook Primary School, Kingswinford

The Witch's Spell

I am the Witch of the West
Making a spell for a pest!
Eyeballs and snakeskin
Mixed together in a rusty old bin,
How he rules the land,
I really do not know,
He should be banned,
From all the land!
He should lie in the sun and die,
I will leave him to fry,
Let him burn,
For all I care,
Let him eat his long, long hair,
Why is he so stupid?
Oh I'll add the thumb of Cupid!
That will make him boiling hot,
I want him to rot!
Smelly socks and toenails,
Ribcages and cats' tails,
I am the best,
Better than all the rest,
Old people's ears and nose hairs,
If he fries nobody cares,
They all care about me, me, me,
They don't even care if they get stung by a bee,
That Princess Lisy,
She is never busy,
I'll get her to make a meeting,
With a very special greeting,
They will die when they walk in,
They will see my dreadful bin!
Then when the prince comes …
He will fry, fry, fry, fry, fry, fry, fry!

Kirby Timmins (10)
Dawley Brook Primary School, Kingswinford

Dear Fairy Godmother

22 Famous Way
Richer Town
Crystalton
XCY PQL

Tuesday 27th June

Dear Fairy Godmother,

    I am complaining to you because I was about to kiss the gorgeous prince when the clock struck twelve. Could you make the spell last until 3am, then I will be able to dance all night. Instead of me running off and losing my glass slipper?

    Have you ever tried running in a frilly ballgown with glass slippers? I nearly broke my ankle. Please may you make the spell last longer.

    Yours sincerely,
    Cinderella.

Philippa Grove
Dawley Brook Primary School, Kingswinford

Dear Council

42 Forest Street
Joe Hampton
Robinson
26.06.06

Dear Council,
    Hansel And Gretel keep eating my house, I'll have none left. My house is completely ruined, it's really annoying because whenever I want to watch TV, there are always crumbs falling on my big black head and I have to shout, 'Get off my roof,' in a loud voice. 'Stop that now you've made a big hole and now you're in another bit.' I have to keep shouting so much I lose my voice and go red! It gives me really bad head energies and feels like my head is going to blow up.
    I like my house the way it is so please can you help me to keep my house nice and well. When you get this letter, please can you help me, you know my address.
Love the Wicked Witch
PS: Please can you help me or else!

Emily Bennett
Dawley Brook Primary School, Kingswinford

Dear Councillor

54 Field Town,
West Midlands,
DY3 GAO
Monday 26th June

Dear Councillor,

    I am writing to complain that the Three Billy Goats Gruff keep annoying me. I want a new bridge so when the Billy Goats Gruff cross it, I won't be annoyed. In my old age I seem to be getting a lot of headaches, the goats aren't helping. Please help me!

    Yours sincerely,
The Big Bad Troll.

Aidan Griffin
Dawley Brook Primary School, Kingswinford

Dear Donkey

>92 Swamp Streets
>Glade Lands
>Disney Parade
>USA

Dear Donkey,

I am writing to you because you are getting on my nerves. You can't come in my house because you wreck the place and you can't stop singing and we cannot live together because we don't get on with each other very well inside. You can come and do stuff outside with me, so will you stop trying to run in my house because I'm trying to get some rest!

Yours sincerely,
From Shrek.

Liam Snape
Dawley Brook Primary School, Kingswinford

Dear Council

36 Sweet Lane
Fairytale Land
West Midlands
DY9 543

Tuesday 27th June

Dear Council,
    I am writing to you to explain that Hansel and Gretel keep on eating my house; they have already eaten my roof, so when it rains candy, my house gets filled with gobstoppers.
    At the moment I'm cleaning out the bathroom after the candy storm last night, and I've got four rooms to go until I'm done.
    They have also eaten my windows and doors and when the candyfloss clouds come, I have to get sticks (chocolate Flakes) to cover the windows and doors. Could you please make them apologise and help me build up the house they ate.
    Yours sincerely,
    The Witch.

Emma Taylor (9)
Dawley Brook Primary School, Kingswinford

Dear Sir

Giant Gardens
Giant World
DY6 8HW

Dear Sir,
I am complaining to you about the other giants trying to eat me and Sophie. Please can you do something about it? Here are some ideas -
Capture them,
Kill them,
Put them in a zoo.
Because I am very busy giving people nice dreams, please try to do something about it.
Yours faithfully,
The BFG.

Jared Whapples (9)
Dawley Brook Primary School, Kingswinford

Dear Billy Goats Gruff Family

28 Bridge Hill
Hill Lane
Goat's Town
West Bridge
Q9B 62H

Monday 26th June 2006

Dear Billy Goats Gruff Family,

I am writing to you to ask if you would mind not walking over my bridge. You see I am very, very old and I need my sleep because I am nocturnal. Maybe you could build a new bridge or ask the council to build one. When you walk across my bridge, I want to eat you. That's why I am writing this letter to you because I can't speak to you or I'll eat you. Please think about it.

Thank you,
T Troll.
(Aka: Tommy Troll)
PS: I stole that piece of chocolate cake under your bed! Sorry!

Selina Garner (9)
Dawley Brook Primary School, Kingswinford

Your Majesty

53 London Street,
Buckingham Grove
England

Your Majesty,
    The three fairies keep changing the colour of my dress from pink to blue and then it all turns multicoloured and when I was dancing, at the ball with the prince, he was very confused because it kept on changing colour.
    They did make a good job of the dress, please tell them to not keep changing the colour of my dress.
Yours sincerely,
Sleeping Beauty.
PS: It's very annoying.

Anna Morris
Dawley Brook Primary School, Kingswinford

The Witch's Spell

With smelly feet and mouldy meat
With frogspawn that's bright
Up over her at night,
I cast a spell over Snow White
I'll make her sleep all day and all night,
To make me bad I rule my life,
The beauty shall be on me,
Hee, hee, hee,
I see you looking good or bad and then
Displaying your thoughts of sad
And you'll have to think and look at me
And then you'll be spooked and taken by me.
Ha ha haaaaaa!

Kay Bennett
Dawley Brook Primary School, Kingswinford

Snow White Sleeping Spell

Boiled frogs' legs
And friend rats' bones
Batwing kebabs,
She will soon be gone.

To make her drop off,
Some steaming hot cocoa
And I will rule my kingdom
Solo!

Ryan Pickin (9)
Fallings Park Primary School, Wolverhampton

Dear Councillor

61 Albert Road
Little Hay
Brickton
BT5 7NJ

27th June 2006

Dear Councillor,
    I am writing to complain about the wall at the corner of Albert Road. I was sitting on the wall having a rest after my long walk when suddenly I landed on the footpath. There was blood pouring from my head and I couldn't move my arm.
    A man was walking past and he tried to help me but I was in too much pain. He called the king's horses and the king's men, they tried their very best to help me, but they couldn't put me back together again. I've spent five weeks in hospital and still feel poorly.
    Please mend the wall before someone else gets injured.
    Yours sincerely,
    Humpty Dumpty.

Phillip Garner (10)
Fallings Park Primary School, Wolverhampton

Jack And Jill Injured

It all began when Jack broke the cold tap in his nan's house, so Jack and Jill had to go up the steep hill to get some water for a cup of tea.

At the top of the hill Jack spilt some of the water and suddenly slipped and Jill followed all the way down the hill. Jack bumped his head on a big massive rock. Then Jill fell on top of him, Jack was knocked out so Jill quickly called 999. The ambulance came like a supersonic rocket and took Jack to hospital. Jill had put vinegar and brown paper on his head but it had not worked!

The doctor told our reporter that Jack was lucky to be alive.

Macaulay Love (10)
Fallings Park Primary School, Wolverhampton

Wake Up!

'Wake up, wake up,'
My stepmom roared,
'Time to do your daily chores!'

I started by sweeping,
The bedroom floor,
When I heard the post
Arrive at the door.

My ugly stepsisters,
Snatched the post,
While I sat and
Ate some toast.

I noticed they were invited
To a grand ball from the prince,
Time for me to go to the mall.

My ugly stepsisters,
Ran upstairs,
To go and see,
What they could wear.

7pm finally came,
My ugly stepsisters
Just looked the same.

When they had gone,
I sat and cried,
'Oh how I wish I could go and hide.'

Puff of smoke,
Glitter and other
And out popped
My fairy godmother.

'You shall go to the ball,'
So she made me a dress,
For once I didn't look such a mess.

My carriage arrived,
'Be back at 12,
Then you will turn back into yourself.'

At the ball I was really shy,
So I sat and ate some pie.

Then the prince,
Asked me to dance,
I said, 'Yes!'
I had a chance!

It soon turned 12
I had to go
Leaving only my glass slipper on show.

Days past,
I was cleaning the floor,
When I heard a knock at the door.

It was the Prince,
He said I was grand,
'May I please take your hand?'

They got married,
Lived at a palace,
With the man she married!

Georgina Jefimik (11)
Fallings Park Primary School, Wolverhampton

Witch's Spell

Crush the toenails,
Cook the bats,
Break the fingers,
Eat the cats
Mix it up with some dogs' ears,
Then when she drinks it,
She'll sleep for years.

Jessie Ansell (9)
Fallings Park Primary School, Wolverhampton

Super Power Kids

It was a new school year for Mark; he had just gone into the classroom when his teacher Miss Cross was announcing that there was a new person in the class, called Daisy. She had short brown hair, blue eyes and a great big smile. Miss Cross said that she should sit next to Mark because she knew that they were both interested in science.

At playtime Daisy came over to Mark and asked to play (she thought he was nice) he wasn't sure but said yes anyway. They really liked each other so the rest of the week, they played together and did their work together. Then on Friday Mark invited Daisy to his lab. (Daisy had been asking to see it all week.)

When they got to the lab, Mark showed Daisy around, she was quite interested until they got to a machine welded to the wall, then she was really interested. It was the 'Super Power Accelerator'. He showed her what it did, then they had some tea and Daisy went home.

That night Daisy didn't feel very well and she couldn't get to sleep, she tossed and turned all night. Then when she got to school the next morning, Mark told her that the reason she didn't feel well was because she had lent against the 'Super Power Accelerator' and that in a few days, she would have super powers.

Mark was right, in a few days, she did get super powers, she got super speed and ran really fast. She told Mark and he said that he had asked his dad about it and he said that they would go in a few weeks, because the machine wasn't quite ready yet, and until a few weeks were over, she would have to hide her powers.

It was hard but she made it.

Naomi Cruden (10)
Ferncumbe CE Primary School, Warwick

Home Alone

'Kids it's time for breakfast!' Then suddenly a wave of them came running down the stairs but they didn't realise that their youngest brother was still asleep. Everyone was packed and ready to go but the neighbour slipped onto the coach without anyone knowing. Carolyn started to count them all including the neighbour, '1, 2, 3, 4, 5, 6, 7, 8, 9, 10, 11, yep that's it all of them.' The neighbour quickly slipped off the coach.

'Mum, Dad anyone home?'

No answer ...

'Cool I made my family disappear!' Dan celebrated by stealing £50 off his biggest brother Ken. Dan spent all his money on food, drink and games.

A day had passed and some robbers were outside waiting in a van.

'Hey which house should we rob first then?' said the smartest robber, Connor.

'Huh what did you say boss?' said the stupidest robber, Toby!

'Just be quiet!' said Connor.

'Hey look what about that house?'

'Yes.' But Dan was prepared for them. *Ding-dong* went the doorbell. Meanwhile back at the airport, 'My son is left on his own!' said Dan's mum dramatically.

Dan was too frightened to open the door so he stuck out a shotgun which fired pellets, *bang* right in the painful but meaningless target. Toby dropped to the floor screaming in pain, 'Oooowwwww!'

'Ha, ha,' laughed Dan.

Connor shouted, 'You are seriously going to pay for that. Wwwoooyyyaaa!' He kicked down the door.

'I'm coming son,' said Dan's mum.

'Ah ha I've got you now,' said Connor.

Neeenor.

'Oh shoot!'

Bang!

'Ah I didn't mean literally, I'm going to get you for that.'

'Freeze in the name of the law.'

'Dang the police caught me red-handed.'

'You're all coming with us.'
'Me as well?'
'Yes you kid.'

'Son you're back, I missed you so much.'
When Dan got home this is what happened.
'Daaaannnn!'

William Dews (10)
Ferncumbe CE Primary School, Warwick

Untitled

'So Doctor where are we going?' I asked.
'We are going to travel 20 years in time,' he replied.
'Which way?'
'Forwards,' he replied.

Suddenly we could hear the universe's noises. There was a loud thump. We had landed. I stepped outside and saw police everywhere. One stared at me and then pulled out his baton, 'Oi you!' he shouted and ran towards me.

Just then the doctor walked out of the Tardis and flashed his sonic screwdriver at him, the man froze. The doctor walked up to him and hit him on the head. 'Metal,' he said.

We walked into the main town. 'Electro binoculars? I thought they were only in Star Wars?' the doctor replied.

Then we came to a school, I looked inside. 'Sliveen!' You could just hear them saying, 'Give us your pencil cases.' I looked around, *where's vinegar?* I thought, then right in front of me was a massive sign, *The Biggest Vinegar Shop In The World.* I ran in and took a bottle of *spray vinegar* and ran to the till and threw £2.50 onto the desk and ran.

The school was 8 metres away, the doctor opened the front door but instead I jumped through the wall and sprayed! Goo went everywhere, then I realised there was a vinegar bomb attached to the side saying *Free With Every Bottle Of Spray Vinegar.* Then millions of Sliveen entered the room, then 8 words came into my head. 'It is time to take out the trash!' and I chucked the grenade! Then there was a swimming pool of goo!

'I think it's time to go,' said the doctor, covered in goo.

Then once again, the universe made its noise.

Charlie Hanson (11)
Ferncumbe CE Primary School, Warwick

The Heart

Have you ever had that feeling where you want something but you don't have anything for it? You feel so frustrated that you want to steal it? Princess Mia had that feeling for something and stole it, and that something was inside her now. She even killed her father for the throne and immediately made herself Queen of the Sea!

The water pixies loved their city until Mia came to the throne. She ordered all pixies to her kingdom and forced them to be slaves and when one single pixie disobeyed her, she whipped them all! The whip was made of rock steel!

So the pixies worked as cooks, cleaners, gold givers and royal guards. Water pixies had scaly gold fins. They did this for many years and all the pixies noticed something very peculiar and mysterious about Queen Mia! She hadn't seemed to age a single day!

All male pixies set out to find out this great mystery and there was one who actually had the courage to go and ask Mia.

'What's your secret to never age?' the pixie said in a tiny voice. Mia looked down at him and she hit him with the cane and he just fell to the floor like he had no bones!

One day, one of the pixies ran into something very peculiar. It was a letter and the letter told the secret of Queen Mia. She'd stolen the heart that never dies from the sea monkey, Jee Jar. He passed the secret onto every pixie in the kingdom. So that night, they set up a plan to steal the heart and that's what they did! A pixie climbed down her throat and grabbed the heart. Mia never woke again.

All the pixies went with the leader of the pixies and returned the heart to the greatest sea monkey of all time. Jee Jar was resurrected.

Simon Wyatt (10)
Ferncumbe CE Primary School, Warwick

Sunshine

Georgia had just moved into her new house. She really wanted a pet dog. Outside Georgia's house was a field and one day she decided to explore so she put on her shoes and headed off. Soon she came across a river, she sat down and leant against a fence. Georgia decided that she liked it there and came after school every day and sat in the same spot.

While she sat there, she thought about dogs and every night, she dreamt about dogs.

One day as usual, Georgia came and sat down against the fence because she had leant against the fence so much, it had become weaker and Georgia fell backwards into the stream. It was very deep and Georgia could not swim.

As she called out for help a golden Labrador pricked up its ears and came bounding over, it pulled her out of the fast flowing water. It licked the water off her face and guided her home.

When Georgia came home with a dog and her clothes all wet, her mum wanted to know what had happened, so while her mum dried her, she told her mum the story of how the dog had saved her life. Georgia became very close friends with the dog and it would not leave her side. The dog had no collar and her mum and dad tried to trace the dog's owner but after two whole weeks, Georgia's mum and dad had had no luck and decided that as long as Georgia looked after the dog, she was allowed to keep it! Georgia was thrilled and called the dog Sunshine.

Charlotte May (10)
Ferncumbe CE Primary School, Warwick

Uncertain Death

The king Duke Platto ordered a platoon of soldiers and the beautiful princess Fiona to go into the deep, dark forest where nobody had gone before. They got saddled up with their sharp crystal-printed swords and rode off into the distance, into Fangorn Forest.

As they rode through the forest, the rain started to pour down with thunder and lightning too. They were just about to turn back when a sudden explosion knocked her horse flat. She rolled clear of the falling hooves and drew her sword but the only enemy was a lightning bolt that had shattered an old oak to splinters.

As they made their way back, a man in a dark cloak was on the path. He told her, 'Follow me and I will give you shelter and warmth.'

The strange man took them up a very steep hill, when they got to the top, there was a dark, gloomy cave. The man took them inside.

She was in the slimy cave, the man had some straw to sit on, she sat down and the man lit a fire, strange shadows flickered around the walls of the cave. She was just about to leave when *slam*, the closing of a door, the fire went out dead.

She heard growling and scratching that made her back shiver with fear, all that was heard was a *scream!*

Joe Edwards (11)
Ferncumbe CE Primary School, Warwick

Untitled

'The Loch Ness! We're not going to the Loch Ness!' shouted Theo.
'Oh yes you are kids,' said Dad,
'Well take you then drop you off,' said Mum.
'We're leaving now, everyone in the car.'
'OK,' said Matt, Theo and Rachel.

They set off to the Loch Ness. An hour later, they arrived. They set up the tent and had some lunch. Mum and Dad left for home.

It became dark and the kids were getting ready for bed when *rrroooaarrr*! A monster from the legend. He was green with yellow spots, razor-sharp teeth and blue eyes. It was indeed the Loch Ness Monster. With its claws the Nessie picked up the tent and threw it sky-high, it landed in a lump of mud. The children screamed, 'Aarrgghh!'

Before the monster could do anything, the kids were racing away at their fastest. The Nessie suddenly started speaking, 'Come back!'

The children were shouting, 'Never!'

The monster was lonely. It just wanted some help because years back there was a war between humans and the Loch Ness. One of the humans threw a spear with a ring on the end at Nessie's mouth and he'd swallowed it and ever since he had been acting badly.

The children were now well ahead of him and by now, they were so tired they needed a rest so they all sat down against a tree and went to sleep.

The next morning when Matt, Theo and Rachel got up and went back to the monster, he was still there just lazing.

Suddenly, *achoo!* The monster sneezed out a ring.
'Maybe the monster was just trying to get help from us,' said Matt.
Vvvvrrrooommm! Mum and Dad's car pulled up.
'Time to go!' shouted Dad.
'But! Dad!' shouted the kids,
'No buts, get in the car!'
'Oh OK.'
'Off we go then,' said Dad.

Connor Ball (10)
Ferncumbe CE Primary School, Warwick

9 More Days Until

9 more days until someone called Callum's birthday. He was so excited. He was watching TV and his mum said, 'Go do your list for your birthday.'

Callum said, 'OK.'

After that Callum went upstairs to get a piece of paper and then went to get the Argos book. Then he wrote down the presents he wanted, then he went to the PlayStation page and thought, *do I want Sims 2 for PlayStation or Nintendo?* He thought and thought and thought and he put it down for the PlayStation and said, '1st best - please get me it ...'

The next day he went to school and the day went like this, he got his books and put them in his bag, then was first in the line for the bus and he said to Mrs Langley, 'It's my birthday in 8 days.'

Mrs Langley said, 'Oooo that's nice, what do you want for your birthday?'

It was Callum's birthday, He was so excited! He got up, woken by all his family so he could open his presents, then he went to school and had a *reallyyyyy* good day. (He really liked that birthday.)

And he loved all the presents he got.

Callum Adams (10)
Ferncumbe CE Primary School, Warwick

Dear Sir/Madam

Dear Sir/Madam

I am writing to explain that I didn't mean to ruin the Three Pigs' homes. You see it was like this ... I was out walking when I saw the Three Pigs' homes and I thought they looked a bit unstable, and as I am an undercover building inspector, it was my duty to see if the houses were safe to live in.

I decided to blow to see if they were stable and, oh no! They fell straight to the ground.

Meanwhile the pigs were inside when all the straw, twigs and bricks fell. I couldn't see and neither could the pigs. My mouth was still open and the pigs thought my mouth was a door and they walked straight into my mouth thinking that it was the open door, and just at that moment, I sneezed and swallowed them whole. I feel so bad that I am now a vegetarian!

Yours sincerely,
Mr Wolf.

Rosie Poliquin-Hill (9)
Manor Way Primary School, Halesowen

Dear Mr Beloved Prince Charming

Dear Mr Beloved Prince Charming,

I am Cinderella's beautiful stepsister, although people accidentally call me 'Ugly'. I am writing to inform you that Cinderella is not that clever, although when she dresses well, she does look a twitchy bit pretty but she is certainly *not* very pretty.

Her cleaning habits are not good, because she doesn't mix fairy soapy liquid into the water so the floors, windows and tiles are not clean. She doesn't finish her 100 chores early so that means she wakes up late, so she doesn't feed the horses, cows and chickens in time so I have to do it.

Pleeeeaaaassse divorce her and marry me! Me! Me! Yes me! I am sooo pretty and cute, not like my twin sister Angelica or Cinderella.

Lots of hugs and kisses

Love from Angelina.

Emily Rose Hill (9)
Manor Way Primary School, Halesowen

Dear Sir/Madam

Dear Sir/Madam,

I didn't mean to blow the pigs' homes down or eat them. I was just walking past a pig's house when I noticed a loose brick in the wall and because I am a building inspector, I had to investigate to make sure the house was safe so I tested the strength of the house by blowing without noticing the pigs on the roof sunbathing.

Suddenly the building collapsed and the pigs on the roof fell. They were going to hit me on the head so as I opened my mouth to scream argh, the pig landed straight into my mouth and I gulped him down, so that's why I shouldn't go to jail.

Yours faithfully
Mr Wolf.

Christian Herbert (9)
Manor Way Primary School, Halesowen

Dear Prince Charming

Dear Prince Charming,

I know that you fell for my sister, but why? She may be a pretty face but there's more to life than that. I know I'm not the prettiest girl in the world but I'm smart, kind, funny, all the things you are. I can cook, juggle and clean. I'd do all the cleaning in the world for you. I've had a row of men at my door asking for me but I've turned them all down. I'm saving myself for you.

Cinderella is mean, did she tell you she put worms in my bed and raw fish in my dressing table drawer! Well she did, she is horrid to me. Why would you want to marry someone like her, she's a clutz! I know the wedding is in three days but the only way you can escape a wedding *disaster* is to say no. I'm not forcing you, *gosh no!* I'm just warning you in advance, she's all the words to describe *evil!*

I make my own clothes, so no clothes shopping for you. I can even make my own bride's dress! I make a gorgeous chocolate soufflé, for all your soufflé needs! (I also make a pretty good pasta!) If you are allergic to anything, tell me and I will never forget! I like short guys and tall guys so if you shrink or grow, I will still love you.

I write poems and I'm especially good at love poems.

Yours sincerely,

Izabell Hoghart.

Laura Nicholson (9)
Manor Way Primary School, Halesowen

Dear Sir/Madam

Dear Sir/Madam,

I am sorry that I ate the Three Little Pigs, I shall explain why I did it.

I was walking along the forest path, enjoying a cool, breezy day. Suddenly, the wind picked up. I sped up to a jog. I sat down to rest on a bench outside a cottage and suddenly there was a large gust of wind, and the house fell down!

Then, three little squealing pigs came running out of the house. Just then, they seemed to freeze. They smelt delicious! I couldn't help myself. I staggered forward and gobbled up the pigs!

I woke up with a start! Phew! The pigs were still alive, or were they? The pigs had disappeared, and my stomach was feeling incredibly full. I worked out what had happened. I had eaten the pigs while sleeping.

So there you are, it was all an accident and besides, even though I ate the pigs, I didn't blow the house down at all!

Yours sincerely,

The Big Good Wolf.

Matthew Bateman (8)
Manor Way Primary School, Halesowen

Dear Giant

Dear Giant,

Jack here! Please come down the beanstalk today. I need to bring something unusual to school. You fit the description perfectly, you're big, you're old, plus scary. Pretty please, say yes.

My teacher is an old bag and I really hate her. I will visit you every day if you do.

From your only mate,

Jack Bean.

PS: How old are you? Please tell at school.

Laura Chui (9)
Oaklands Primary School, Birmingham

Daisy

Miss Clarke looked out of the window and called for her husband. 'See next door, there are daisies growing. I have not seen any for years. Please pick some for me,' she said.

Her husband clambered over the wall and was about to pick the daisies when he heard a voice behind him.

'Hey you over there, pick them flowers and gimme ya first child,' it said. The man didn't think it likely he'd have a child so he picked the flowers and ran.

About ten months later, Miss Clarke had a little baby girl and the witch came. She snatched the baby from its cot and fled. The witch named her Daisy.

When Daisy was sixteen, the witch locked her in a tower. Every morning when she woke up the witch sang, 'Daisy, Daisy, let down your fair hair,' and Daisy would let down her long blonde hair.

One day a passing prince head the chant and decided to try it out. So when the witch went inside, he did and after that he went every day.

But one day Daisy said, 'Why can't you climb any faster, like the prince?' to the witch.

The witch moved Daisy to the other side of the world, when the prince came, she jumped onto him and he went blind.

The prince searched across the world for Daisy and soon found her. Magically the love of Daisy gave the prince his eyesight. They got married and lived happily ever after.

Aqeela Zafar (10)
Oaklands Primary School, Birmingham

Cinderella

Once upon a time there was a girl named Kelly. Kelly lived with her stepmother and her two daughters Molly and Polly. Molly and Polly took Kelly's clothes for themselves and dressed Kelly in rags. Kelly's evil stepmother ordered her to cook and clean and her new name was Cinderella.

One day when the sun was shining, the king's youngest son was celebrating his eighteenth birthday by throwing a ball. Everybody got an invitation including the two sisters and Cinderella. Cinderella pleaded with her stepmother to give permission but she growled no and sent her to her room.

Cinderella was in her room crying. She could not understand why she did not have permission to go to the biggest party of the year! Suddenly a light filled the room and blinded Cindy and a fairy plopped down on the floor. 'You shall go to that ball,' said the fairy and suddenly Cindy was in a beautiful silky white dress.

The fairy whisked Cindy to the ball.

'May I have this dance?' said a voice and it was the prince. The prince took Cindy's hand and they danced all night.

Suddenly Cinderella vanished before the prince's eyes but the prince managed to grab her shoe …

The prince searched all night, he searched every home until he got to Cinderella's house. The sisters argued about who was the mystery person but the prince put the shoe on Cinderella's foot. The prince proposed to Cinderella and they lived happily ever after.

Tia Brown (10)
Oaklands Primary School, Birmingham

Cinderella

Once upon a time a girl called Cinderella lived in a flat in the middle of the city with her two ugly stepsisters.

Cinderella went to school but everyone ignored her.

Whilst she was at home, she washed the dishes, washed the clothes and scrubbed the floor.

One day her friend invited her to the school disco but her sisters said she couldn't go to the disco. Cinderella was in her room when a fairy came whizzing through the window.

Cinderella was amazed. 'Who are you?'

'I'm your fairy, I'm here to make your wishes come true.'

'I want to go to a disco and look pretty.'

Cinderella really wanted to go to the disco because Chris was there from Year 8.

By 6pm Cinderella was at the disco but by 9.30pm she had to go home or else she would go back to her normal self.

The clock was ticking by, 6.40pm, everyone was there dancing. She was having so much fun that she lost track of time. When she looked at her watch she ran out of the door as quick as she could.

But she dropped her mobile on the floor and Chris picked it up and followed her home. 'Cinderella,' said Chris.

Cinderella stopped walking and turned around. 'I have found your mobile.'

'Ah thanks,' said Cinderella.

From that day on Cinderella and Chris lived happily ever after.

Faith Scanlon (10)
Oaklands Primary School, Birmingham

The Food Zapper!

On one gloomy, dreary, dark morning in a small town called Kelake there was an intelligent girl named Grace. As Grace awoke, she noticed the miserable weather outside, she felt extremely cold inside. Grace got out of bed and went downstairs into the kitchen and made herself some breakfast. She turned on the TV and watched a news report on NASA's new rocket.

She felt inspired - straight after her breakfast, she got dressed and hurried to her workshop where she began to build a rocket! It took many hours but eventually she had finished. She decided to test it, so into the garden she went, then suddenly ... *Boom!* She landed on a small planet without outer space! She stepped out of her rocket. Meanwhile noticing she was on Planet Mars!

Grace looked around observing the tiny multicoloured huts. Suddenly a small alien appeared. On the side of him there were more aliens hard at work. This alien noticed Grace looking at the hard working aliens and mumbled, 'Planet Jupiter rules us, we have to give them food, if not they will destroy us, but we had a climate change so the food will not grow!'

Grace replied, 'I have this food zapper. It makes as much food as possible, I invented it myself.'

So off Grace went to the rocket and brought the food zapper towards them. She exclaimed, 'Stand back.' She then pressed the button and a huge, enormous, colossal pile of food appeared. All the aliens rushed over and repeatedly said, 'Thank you.'

Proudly Grace went back to her rocket and turned the key, however the engine would not start. How will she ever get home?

Helen Mockler (10)
Our Lady of Lourdes Primary School, Birmingham

Death In The Undergrowth

The big tragedy began one morning that seemed to be a normal day for me, Gerald the grasshopper, but as the day progressed, I would see how wrong I was! It started as a normal day with me getting ready for the annual work festival.

I set out with a lifted spirit, which quickly sank at the sight that met my eyes. There was nothing but war, destruction and endless meteors in all directions. I was so enticed with my big work festival that I forgot that it was the mating season! The sad thing is that all this is just to earn the right to mate.

The rhinoceros beetles were flinging each other as if they were both immensely strong (lightweight) cushions. Mantises everywhere were lashing out and slashing each other then, that's when I saw him ... my challenge.

Instantly, my instincts kicked in, blocking my usually peaceful self from the battlefield. This year, I was going to make if it was the last thing I did! So the epic battle raged as we thrust our powerful hind legs at each other. Finally I summoned up all my remaining strength and put it all into one last kick which threw my rival against the nearest grass blade.

That ... was when the Emperor dragonflies made their extravagant entrance, this was the fight that everyone had been waiting to watch. The dragonflies began to hustle into the dance of death, after hours of dangerous pirouetting, one dragonfly lifelessly fluttered to the surface of the pond.

Then, as if by magic, the barren battlefield was transformed into a church hall filled with millions of: 'I dos.' That's how I ended up here, in my big house, with a beautiful wife as well as three perfect kids. What more could a bug want?

Alessandro Barwani-Rai (10)
Our Lady of Lourdes Primary School, Birmingham

Asking For An Apology!

Red Street
Cake
BO6 RRL

Warty Peak Lane
Wolfy Hill
BBW W66

Dear Little Red Riding Hood,
    I am writing to complain about your cake making skills. The other day when I was lying in bed dressed as your grandma, I took a peek in your bag and I couldn't resist your mouth-watering cakes!
    So, I took a large bite of your dotty cakes and fell asleep. I woke up with anger, as I looked in the mirror! I had grown wo-spots on my face.
    They were horrible, fat, red, wo-spots. After a while, I had calmed down and decided to go to a wo-doctor, (a specialist doctor of wolves), as I trotted down the hills, I was filled with embarrassment. The wo-doctor said that I had got wo-spots because of some food I had eaten. The wo-doctor gave me information about the food, it had coloured dots on it and it was ... poisoned!
    Then it occurred in my mind. Cakes! Someone had given me cakes and it was you Little Red Riding Hood, so I would like an apology from you.
    I have some suggestions:
    Bring me some nice cakes,
    Get me some wo-cream, for protection.

If you don't apologise, you wouldn't like to catch my spots.
    Yours sincerely,
    Wolfy.

Lubna Amir (10)
Our Lady of Lourdes Primary School, Birmingham

How I Wished I Was Not Scared Of ...

My legs trembled and I felt an icy shimmer up my spine; impetuously my stomach circled into a dance of sadness, edging closer ...
'Argh!'
With an almighty rumpus I dived out of the way, and was relieved to see my dad put a cup above the spider.

Conor Burns (10)
Our Lady of Lourdes Primary School, Birmingham

The Millionaire Runaway!

In the gloomy, rainy streets of London, there lived a young typical eleven-year-old girl called Maria. She lived with her concerning mother who didn't even let her go to school on her own! Maria was a very unlucky girl who always wished for a different change in her life ...

Maria's mum was always hoping her numbers would come up on the lottery. Obviously they didn't.

'Maria, come downstairs, Mummy wants you to go to the shop.'

Henceforth, Maria went to the shop with her mother holding her hand firmly.

'Right, pick some lottery numbers for me,' asked Maria's mother.

Within minutes, Maria had chosen the numbers, her mum had paid a pound and they were on their way home. (They were in a rush as the lottery was about to start.) It was bad luck; none of Maria's numbers came up. Fortunately, Maria had spotted that she had done a different type of lottery than the one on the television.

That night, Maria phoned the lottery hotline to check her numbers.

'I've won! *I really have!*' cried Maria. She had unbelievably won! Millions of pounds were hers. Being it was night, Maria tiptoed upstairs to pack all her clothes and camped outside the lottery collection point. As soon as it was open, she literally grabbed her money and ran away to be free from her concerning mother!

Natalie Rahill (10)
Our Lady of Lourdes Primary School, Birmingham

Papa Bear!

Dear Papa Bear,

I am writing to inform you about the porridge because it has run out, you'll have to get more for me to eat! I suppose you couldn't do me a favour and get a comfy chair, and a better bed. Oh of course, I nearly forgot, I am moving in and I'll bring my stuff at 6pm sharp, if you want to throw me out talk to my lawyer.

See you later!
Goldilocks.

Zoe Tubb (10)
Our Lady of Lourdes Primary School, Birmingham

Dear Snow White

Dear Snow White,

I am writing to you to complain about the noise level that you have been making twenty-four hours a day. I am very appalled that I have to tell people who visit me, that I am busy! I don't like lying and I am lying. In fact it is beyond appalling. I am going to carry this into the hands of the police if you do not keep the noise down which is completely unnecessary.

Yours sincerely,
Cinderella.
PS: Also quit the singing!

Katie Rosina Warren (10)
Our Lady of Lourdes Primary School, Birmingham

Savagers!

One scorching, roasting day a group of pirates soared through the waves of the ferocious sea. The crew were named the Savagers. Their proper names were Legged (the captain) he had short curly black hair with a bushy beard. There was another shipmate named Minky (he is the funny one!) Minky was bald and was always messing about. Last but not least Stinky (he was the moody one as a result he didn't get on with Minky). Stinky had blond hair as well as ghastly eyebrows! As you can imagine, they're a crazy lot!

They set off for the Caribbean but they had one problem ... they didn't know how to get there.

'Move over Minky!' Stinky grunted,
'No! I don't want to,' replied Minky,
'Would you two just be quiet?' Legged complained,
'Yes Captain!' they both answered, they all sat there doing nothing, they were extremely bored.
'Are we there yet?' asked Minky,
'Nooo!' boomed Legged,
'Captain, Captain!' shouted Stinky,
'What now?' replied Legged,
'We're here!' Stinky screamed with joy.

Legged was so ecstatic. He walked over to Minky and Stinky and heaved them over deck. 'Bye-bye!' Legged shouted cheerfully as he sailed off into the sunset!

Jade Amanda Crosbee (10)
Our Lady of Lourdes Primary School, Birmingham

Bats, Witches, Eyes

B ats, witches and eyes,
A re full of surprise,
T ake the bat,
S tir together.

W atch out for the witch, she brings bad weather,
I will get it finished, I know I will,
T aking your time, keeping really still,
C atching the frogs,
H ike down to the bogs.

E yes watering,
Y elling for help,
E ating up the potion that's making you yelp!

Laura Patricia Horton (10)
Our Lady of Lourdes Primary School, Birmingham

The Dragons' Football Day Out

There were five little dragons all named by numbers. The littlest dragon number five was very hungry, so he decided to wake up his other brothers and sisters, so they could all go and get something to eat together. He woke number four up and number four woke number three up, then number three woke number two and at last number two woke number one up.

Number five called out, 'Can we all go and have a nibble on some toast?'

'Yes but it's morning anyway!' gasped number two.

Today's the big day for England,' roared number four.

'Breakfast time,' called Mother.

They all agreed that breakfast was lovely and when every last crumb was gone, their dad called them to go to the England football game, they were also going to meet some football players.

Dragon number one had bought a present for Steven Gerrard, dragon number two had bought a present for Peter Crouch, dragon number three had bought a present for Wayne Rooney, number four had bought one for Joe Cole and number five had made a very special box of cookies for Ashley Cole. When they went to the match, little dragon number five had bought his present and gave it to Ashley Cole. In return he gave him his football shirt.

Later they went to the football match and watched England play, the dragons were shouting, 'Five dragons on a shirt!'

By the end the score was 2-1 against Sweden. England's last game and they won the World Cup.

England are great!

Christine Cartlidge (10)
Our Lady of Lourdes Primary School, Birmingham

Fairy Tale (Chair Tragedy)

It was a cold day in the three bear's house so they made some porridge. While it was in the pot, Little Bear suggested to go for a walk. They wrapped up warm and set off into the woods. They were gone a while so the porridge was probably cold by now.

After a good 15 minutes walk, they decided to head home, when they got home, something was wrong but the three bears didn't know it yet.

All three of them sat down to eat their porridge, when Baby Bear went to sit down, he fell on the floor. He looked up and found his chair was gone. Then behind them, crept the big bad wolf.

Daddy Bear quickly threw his chair at the wolf's head and the wolf never dared come back again, or did he?

Ciarán McCarthy (10)
Our Lady of Lourdes Primary School, Birmingham

The World Cup Final

As I stepped out of the tunnel, I could hear all the fans chanting my name in the World Cup Final in Berlin. I was brilliant, it was England Vs Brazil and we were going to win by 5 goals to nil. I was going to score them all.

Regan Rowley (10)
Our Lady of Lourdes Primary School, Birmingham

Nursery Rhymes

Slugs and snails,
Puppy-dogs' tails,
I'll get that Snow White,
I might have a fight,
But I'll kill her at last,
It will be such a blast,
Then she'll go to Heaven,
With the lucky number seven,
Strapped to her chest,
I'll be the best,
Now they'll see,
They'll be growling at me,
My name might not be Pular,
But I'll still be a ruler.

Emily Treacy (10)
Our Lady of Lourdes Primary School, Birmingham

Cindybella

Far away in a kingdom, lived a girl named Cindybella. She lived with her ugly sisters in an old house.

One day a letter arrived for Cindybella. The ugly sisters snatched it from Cindybella's hand. It said:

'Dear Miss,

I have invited you to my ball. The prettiest woman will marry me.

Prince'.

The ugly sisters were so excited, they made a list for Cindybella so she could get what they needed, so she did. The two ugly sisters went off to the ball leaving Cindybella alone.

In a minute, the fairy godfather appeared. Cindybella knew he was the fairy godfather. He asked Cindybella what happened, so she told him. The fairy clicked his fingers and the white glamorous tablecloth turned into a silky dress. From the corner of her eye, there appeared glass slippers, a unicorn and a pair of gloves.

At 9.00 she had to come back. Cindybella sat on the unicorn and went to the ball. When she arrived, she danced with the prince and the two ugly sisters were jealous.

When it was 9.00 she ran out and dropped her glove. The prince saw it. He went round to everyone's houses to try it on, but it did not fit anyone. When he went to Cindybella's house, the two ugly sisters tried it on first but it did not fit. When Cindybella tried it, it fitted.

The prince and Cindybella got married and lived happily ever after.

Nagina Kauser (10)
Palfrey Junior School, Walsall

The Gingerbread Man

Dear Sir and Madam,

I have tried to bake your gingerbread man back together but he just keeps falling apart. I have tried sticking back on the gumdrop buttons, I have tried pouring milk and water on him but it just does not work. Shall I try beating him together?

I shall be in a very good mood if this does work as I'm in a very bad mood at the moment as everything I try goes wrong.

So last night, I heard owls in the garden trying to get in so I chucked a bit of cold water at them. I managed to stop the owl but I don't have anymore ideas, what shall I do, come down to the bakery on Sunday morning?

Yours hopefully,
M Baker.

Mitchell Pettifor (10)
Palfrey Junior School, Walsall

Little Violet Violent Head

It was a hot summer's day in Wales. The wolf family were getting ready to go and bathe in the sea. Little Wolf and Mama Wolf were ready so Mama Wolf said to Little Wolf to go and give her grandad some fruit.

Off she went with one Sharon fruit, two mandarins, two mangoes, four grapefruits, seven peaches all in a basket. She did not see that Little Violet Violent Head was following her.

When they got to a clearing Little Violet Violent Head ran to the back of Grandad's house and punched Grandad who was just about to open the front door and shoved him underneath his bed. It was easy because Grandad lived in a bungalow and because she was violent. Then she quickly dressed up in Grandad's clothes and sat in bed waiting for Little Wolf to knock on the door.

Suddenly there was a knock on the door, 'Come in,' said Little Violet Violent Head in a sweet voice. Then the door gave a creak and opened, 'Oh, what small eyes you have!' said Little Wolf.

'All the better to see you with,' said Little Violet Violent Head.

'What small teeth you have,'

'All the better to eat you with.'

And Little Violet Violent Head jumped out of bed and ate Little Wolf. Suddenly Little Violet Violent Head heard shouts of anger and Little Wolf's dad Mr Wolf came in with a big piece of strong rope and tied up Little Violet Violent Head and threw her into a barn shed. Then Violet got violent and at last fought her way through and ran away. She was never ever seen again but if she was, she was always found wearing a red cape that she had stolen from Little Wolf's grandad's house and she always claimed herself to be *Little Red Riding Hood*.

Muhammad Patas (9)
Palfrey Junior School, Walsall

Goldilocks And The Three Bears

One morning, Daddy Bear, Mummy Bear and Baby Bear went for a walk. Goldilocks went into the three bear's house. Goldilocks was hungry so she had some porridge. She had Baby Bear's porridge, it was too salty. Then she saw Mummy Bear's porridge, it was too sweet. Then she saw Daddy Bear's porridge, it was just right and she ate it.

Goldilocks looked for a chair, Baby Bear's chair was too small, Mummy Bear's chair was too soft, Daddy Bear's chair was just right.

Goldilocks was sleepy so she went upstairs. Baby Bear's bed was too small, Mummy Bear's bed was too soft, Daddy Bear's bed was just right.

Then the three bears came home.

'Who's been eating my porridge and who put the porridge in my chair?' said Daddy Bear.

The three bears were sleepy so they went upstairs and Daddy Bear said, 'There is Goldilocks. Let's make a witch's spell!' And this is what the three bears said, 'Make Goldilocks not come to our house.'

Goldilocks never came back and the three bears lived happily ever after.

Faiz Ahamad (8)
Palfrey Junior School, Walsall

Hansel And Gretel

Once there was a girl and a boy called Hansel and Gretel, their mother was nice but when she got angry, she was mean. Their father was not friendly either.

One day Hansel heard his father say 'Take the children in the forest and leave them there.' When Hansel heard this, he told Gretel, then he got some bread and when they left Hansel put a trail of bread from their house to the forest. Their parents left them.

Hansel felt cold and smelt ice cream, they came close to the house made out of chocolate ice cream and started eating all the ice cream, then an old lady came out.

The old woman said, 'Come in, I have got some more different flavoured ice cream.' She said it in a funny way.

Hansel went inside the ice cream house and Gretel stayed outside. Hansel was stuffed from eating all the ice cream. 'Oh, I'm stuffed, I shouldn't eat that much ice cream,' said Hansel, then the old lady came and grabbed Hansel and put him in a cage. 'Ha! Ha! Ha!' she said.

'You are not just an old lady, you are a witch,' he said. 'Help!'

Gretel heard someone say help, she looked in the window and it was Hansel. 'I've got to get him,' she said.

Gretel knocked on the door and hid when the old lady came out, she went round the house to see who the person knocking was, then Gretel went inside and opened the cage.

Hansel came out of the cage and they opened the window and ran away. They found the bread and followed the tracks and went back home.

Mahfuja Akthar (9)
Palfrey Junior School, Walsall

Aladdin

Princess Sindy was having a great time with Aladdin. One day the genie got so jealous that he turned Aladdin into a fat ugly man and he turned himself into a handsome man. Sindy started to hang about with the genie and she forgot about Aladdin.

So many times Aladdin always begged the genie but the genie refused him.

One year went by Aladdin was poor, when he tried to steal food he always got caught.

One day the princess got married to the genie and lots of people settled down to start the ceremony. Then came Aladdin to stop the marriage. Aladdin said, 'He's a genie!' Lots of people were furious. Then the flying carpet and the monkey came to Aladdin.

The princess' uncle shouted, 'That's Aladdin,' then the people were shocked. The genie tried to run away. Aladdin grabbed him and said, 'Turn me back to who I was before.' This time the genie couldn't say no. He turned Aladdin back to who he was and he turned himself back too.

The princess and Aladdin lived happily ever after.

Shahed Miah (9)
Palfrey Junior School, Walsall

Cindafella

There once lived a girl called Cindafella. Her mother and father died. She was very upset and sad so she had to live with her older sisters, who were very kind.

One day when they woke up they got out of bed, then went to the bathroom and brushed their teeth, then went downstairs. When they got down, they saw the mail, they got it and started reading it, there was a party at their auntie's.

When they reached their auntie's house, the went inside, sat down and had the party and then stayed for a sleepover. While they were there, they had fun and lived happily ever after.

Hamima (9)
Palfrey Junior School, Walsall

Beauty And The Seven Dwarves

Once upon a time there was a mother, she had a child. When it was seven, she passed away. She named her child Beauty because she was beautiful. Her dad had a magic mirror which told how beautiful he was. After a while, Dad married a nice lady, Beauty loved her a lot, and the stepmother also loved her a lot.

Dad asked the mirror his normal question, it said 'Your wife and Beauty are better looking than you.' He shrieked with fury and ordered them both to be killed. When they heard this, they ran away themselves.

They came to a house, the mother knocked on the door and said kindly, 'Please can we stay?' Inside was a friendly giant and seven dwarves who welcomed them kindly.

Meanwhile Dad asked the mirror where they were, the mirror never lied and told him. He bought an axe to kill them. In the house they didn't have an axe and the giant was too friendly to do anything and the dwarves would never attack anyone so they called the big, good wolf, he shot the dad.

And they all lived happily ever after in the little house.

Haleema Lorgat
Palfrey Junior School, Walsall

Agony Aunt's Letter Of The Week

Dear Agony Aunt,
    Last week I heard my stepmother say a little spell, a bit like this:
'Gruesome eyeballs
and muddy mud,
worms and slugs for Snow White's lunch,
a crushed sleeping pill,
I shall make her kip,
Then my woodcutter shall take her to the end of the forest,
And cut out her heart,
Then within a minute, I shall eat her heart,
Then we shall see who is most pretty.'

Oh Agony Aunt, what shall I do?
    From Anonymous (Snow White)

Moaaza Nadat
Palfrey Junior School, Walsall

Evil Cinderella

Many years ago in a faraway land there lived a girl named Cinderella. She had two stepsisters, who were gentle and kind to others. On the other hand, Cinderella was evil and didn't care at all. Every day Cinderella would get up and go to her stepsisters' room and put all sorts of things in their bed like snails, caterpillars and slugs.

After that the stepsisters would get up and start screaming, yelling and calling, 'Cinderella, Cinderella, Cinderella, get here now!'

After a few nights, Cinderella kept an eye on the stepsisters. If they didn't do it, they would be sent to the dungeon where all the mice and rats build their nests to live. Every morning and night Cinderella would go and see if the stepsisters were doing what they had been told by Cinderella.

Several weeks later, everything started to change with Cinderella when she kept giving them things to do. The stepsisters clicked their fingers, to call the wizard to help them. The stepsisters said, 'What's happening to Cinderella?'

'I'm doing it,' said the wizard to the stepsisters.

The stepsisters said, 'I'm your best friend,' and Cinderella said that 'I'm your friend now.' The wizard was very joyful with himself and they lived happy ever after.

Annie Marie Grainger (10)
Palfrey Junior School, Walsall

Cinderella's Fairy Godmother's Diary

Monday 23rd

Dear Diary,
 I am disgusted in the way Cinderella treats those girls, she should not be allowed to go to the ball. She has been such a pain ever since her mother has died, that goes for her father as well.

Saturday 28th

Dear Diary,
 Today is the day before the ball, Cinderella has been making those girls work so hard lately. I don't know why she's bothering because they have no proper clothes, never mind ballgowns!

Sunday 29th

Dear Diary,
 Today is the day of the ball, Cinderella left a few moments ago, she didn't let her stepsisters go though. I'll soon put a stop to that! I hope they return by midnight.

Monday 30th

Dear Diary,
 Cinderella has found out that they were at the ball.

Wednesday 1st June

Dear Diary,
 Cinderella has killed the stepsisters, that nasty girl! Cinderella is now married to the prince, I don't know how it happened but it did.

Thursday 9th

Dear Diary,
 Something absolutely outrageous has happened. Cinderella has murdered the royal family.

Friday 10th

Dear Diary,
 The whole kingdom is now under the power of Queen Cinderella. Everyone is suffering. She has even buried her stepmother, alive! Can anybody save us?

Saturday 14th July

Dear Diary,

A queen from a neighbouring country has killed Cinderella. The two kingdoms are overjoyed and have celebrated for days. The best thing is the queen has killed two evil queens, Cinderella is actually Snow White's stepmother. She had poisoned the royal family with apple pie. I bet you're wondering who the queen who saved us is. She is Snow White! This is the last entry I will make because Cinderella is dead.

Nazeerah Zainab Akbar (9)
Palfrey Junior School, Walsall

Snow White's Father

There was once a king, he wanted a wife who was as delicate as a rose.

He searched every town and village, one after another, but the poor old king couldn't find the perfect one.

One Saturday night, there was a knock on the door, *bang! Bang!*

Two servants scurried to the wooden door, they invited in the mysterious stranger, the king took one look at the visitor, and his heart started racing in and out.

There was a deep silence, then suddenly ... he screamed. 'You're the one, my beautiful lady!'

The woman gave a cruel smile and she said, 'So where is my crown, my dear husband?'

Papiya Begum (10)
Palfrey Junior School, Walsall

The Three Little Wolves And The Big Hairy Pig

Once upon a time deep in the woods, lived three wolves, who were very kind and gentle. They had become a lot more mature now and were able to look after themselves, so they moved out, each building their own house.

The only bad and unfortunate thing about it was; that there lived a big bad pig that destroyed every house he saw. The pig came to the first wolf's house, 'Let me come in right now!' yelled the pig.

'Go home Pig,' replied the wolf.

'No I won't, not on the hair on my hairy hair beard,' said the pig and he bulldozed the brick house down. Luckily, the wolf escaped to the second wolf's house before he could get harmed.

'Let me in wolves!' said the pig.

'Go home Pig,' replied the wolves.

'No, I won't, not on the hair on my hairy hair beard.'

And the pig burnt the wooden house down. Luckily the wolves escaped before harm could be done. They moved to the third wolf's house.

'Let me in wolves,' said the pig. 'I've had enough, you are on my land.'

'Go home Pig,' chorused the wolves.

'No I won't, not on the hair on my hairy hair beard.'

And before the pig could do anything, the youngest sibling pulled out a blaster and shot the pig. The pig was no more, and all three wolves lived happily ever after.

Mohammed Kasujee (11)
Palfrey Junior School, Walsall

Cinderella

There once lived a girl named Cinderella, as I mention her name I tremble, as you know her mother had died and now her father needed to get married, so her father married a nasty, beautiful but clever lady named Camila. Camila had 2 daughters named Anastasia and Drizella. They were both kind and gentle. Camila made Anastasia and Drizella obey Cinderella who was mean and ugly and Camila only loved Cinderella.

Camila read a letter out to all of them one day, it said, 'Dear house owner, I invite you to the princess' ball at which the prince will choose his princess. Come in your best gowns and tiaras. Yours faithfully the king.'

Then Camila called for her daughters to make Cinderella the most beautiful and loveliest lady in the world. Anastasia and Drizella were told to give their beautiful dresses/gowns to Cinderella and Cinderella was told to give her nasty old rags to her sisters and when they were all told to put their clothes on, Cinderella started to tease Anastasia and Drizella and just then the door creaked open and …

But I bet you're wondering what happened to Cinderella, well she did marry the prince but he divorced her and cursed her which turned her into an ass, he married her sisters and executed Camila and their father lived happily ever after with the king.

Zakirah Kalang (10)
Palfrey Junior School, Walsall

Little Red Riding Hood

Once there was a little girl who liked to visit her poorly grandma, she had shiny hair, twinkly eyes, pinky cheeks and rosebud lips. She was known as 'Red Riding Hood' because of the cloak she always wore.

She was so pretty that everyone who saw her thought she was as sweet as a cup of tea with twelve sugars in it. No one noticed that she had an enormous tattoo of a dragon on her arm.

As she was going to her grandma's, she found a hill covered in daisies. She thought it would be lovely to pick some to cheer old granny up.

Meanwhile, poor little grandma was sleeping when a dreadful wolf burst open the door. He was going to eat her but he thought her flesh looked tough so he threw her out of the window and she fell into the river and drowned. He thought he might wait for Red Riding Hood instead.

As the little girl, clutching some daisies, knocked on her grandma's door, the wolf licked his lips. Unfortunately he did not know that ever since she had seen 'Shanghai Noon', with Jackie Chan, she had been obsessed with kung fu fighting. When she saw the wolf, she did a flying kick to his chest and chopped so hard that his neck broke in 3 places.

So the moral of this story is that appearances can be deceptive.

Asiya Tahar (10)
Palfrey Junior School, Walsall

Cinderella

Cinderella was mean and nasty even then her father really loved her. After her mother died, Cinderella's father married again. Her stepmother had two pretty daughters, Anastasia and Drizella. Cinderella's father died after a few days.

Cinderella stopped being nice and started to be cruel and mean to her sisters. Anastasia and Drizella were servants in their own home.

An invitation came to the house saying that there was going to be a ball, everyone was excited.

The coach arrived to take Cinderella and her sister to the ball. The prince danced with Anastasia, when the clock struck twelve, Anastasia and Drizella became bad. Cinderella became good. Anastasia's ring fell off. The prince found it and said, 'Whoever this ring fits they will be my bride.'

So the next day the prince went to everyone's house. They finally came to Cinderella's house, he tried it on Anastasia, 'It fits,' she cried.

The prince got married on the day, Cinderella got married to a beekeeper that collected honey.

Drizella didn't get married but wanted to stay with her mother, she wanted to stay there because her mother was rich.

Rahena Begum (10)
Palfrey Junior School, Walsall

Cinderella And The Modern Day Prince

As I said last time, they lived happily ever after, well that isn't exactly what happened. There were (like most relationships) the ups and the downs, but the thing that made the most difference was that unlike Cinderella, Prince Charming was a modern-day fanatic.

I shall now give you an example, Cinderella insisted on brooms, while Prince Charming insisted on a vacuum cleaner. Cinderella insisted on theatres and her husband wanted the cinema.

But there were things that they did agree on, food and vacations. They often went on vacations because they made a promise to go and either do everything old old-fashioned or vice verse. They also liked the same food so they never argued about that.

Now to the main story, I'm going to keep it short so those people who don't like reading big novels, don't worry. It's about their first vacation and they had decided it was going to be modern day. They went to Disney Land Resort, Florida for two weeks. While they went Old King Charming was put in charge of the country (once again!) They went to America on American Airlines in first class, and then to the Resort in a limousine. They spent most of their time on attractions and sleeping and a bit of time eating and washing.

They had a wonderful time and when they got home, it started all over again. The fight between old and new, (except for food of course).

Ahmed Ali Tarajia
Palfrey Junior School, Walsall

Fantasy

One day there was a gorgeous-looking girl named Snow White, she lived in a little bungalow with her stepmother, her stepmother was so cruel just because Snow White was a pretty girl. Snow White's stepmother could not stand the sight of the poor girl. She kicked Snow White out with Snow White's things. The cruel thing (old bag) said to Snow White, 'You get out you rotten old nag!' so she did but Snow White found a portal.

Snow White went inside the portal and said in a sweet voice, 'I hope I find a nice place, and a handsome man to go with it!' It took about 15 minutes through the portal. She said, 'Oh, oh what a lovely place,' in an outstanding voice. 'Gosh look at the beautiful flowers,' said Snow White. Snow White went and smelt the flowers, she had this feeling inside her, she fainted from the scented flowers.

This prince came on a horse and saw Snow White and said in a manly voice, 'Golly, gulp and gosh!'

The prince really fancied Snow White and gave her a beautiful light kiss.

Eventually Snow White woke up and said, 'Oh my who are you?'

The prince said, 'I am your only true love.'

They gazed into each other's eyes and said together, 'I love you' and lived happily ever after.

Sonia Waheed (10)
Palfrey Junior School, Walsall

Cinderella

Cinderella was mean and nasty, even then her father liked her. After her mother died, her father married again. Her stepmother had two daughters named Drizella and Anastasia. They were really kind. After her father died, she started to treat her sisters and stepmother like slaves. Then a message came and it said, 'The prince is looking for a wife and everyone is to attend.' Cinderella read it and went to get ready.

When the coach came for Cinderella, she went to the ball and while her sisters were cleaning a fairy swooped down and whispered, 'You each get a wish.' They wished to go to the ball and the fairy granted their wish.

They got to the ball and saw Cinderella. At that moment, Cinderella turned kind and her sisters turned mean and nasty. Cinderella saw them and ran home. She left her ring behind. The prince said, 'Whoever the ring fits will be my wife.' So he went out and looked for his future wife and while Cinderella was cleaning, he came to the door, her sisters told her to open the door, he came in and tried it on Anastasia and it was too big. He tried it on Drizella, she screamed, 'It fits, it fits.'

He did not want to get married to her so he pulled and pulled then eventually it came off. He tried it on Cinderella and it fitted perfectly and they got married. Anastasia and Drizella got married to the prince's brothers.

Juleka Begum (9)
Palfrey Junior School, Walsall

Story Of Cinderella

Once upon a time, there was a girl called Cinderella. She was getting ready for the prince's ball. She said, 'What shall I wear?' then a fairy godmother came and gave her a dress, just like the little shining stars in the sky.

She reached the ball and danced with the prince till 12 o'clock. At 12 she ran away and left her glass slipper.

The prince went to find the person that the shoe would fit. He was going to marry her. The prince tried the glass slipper on Cinderella's sisters, but it did not fit them. Then Cinderella came to try on the shoe. She said, 'This is my shoe.'

She showed the other one, she tried the glass slipper and it fitted her.

They both got married and they lived happily ever after. The ugly sisters were never seen again.

Tayabah Kanwel (10)
Palfrey Junior School, Walsall

Snow White The Evil Girl

Once there was an evil girl called Snow White. She had a mirror. Every day she would look in and say, 'Mirror mirror on the wall, who is the fairest of us all?' Every day the answer was the same but one day it said, 'You are second, the queen is the fairest of us all.'

'Argh!' Snow White had an idea, she put poison in the queen's food, oh no! Snow White ate the poison. The queen had the mirror and lived happily ever after!

Jumanah Kasujee (8)
Palfrey Junior School, Walsall

Letter To Agony Fairy

I am writing to tell you that my two ugly stepsisters and my cruel, nasty and disgraceful stepmother are driving me crazy!

My two ugly stepsisters are so lazy. They keep on saying, 'Cinderella get me a cup of coffee. Cinderella get me a bowl of soup, and blah, blah, blah …'

They always wear pretty and clean clothes but they make me wear dirty and disgusting clothes. My stepsisters and my stepmother hate me because I'm nice, beautiful and charming!

My nasty, cruel and disgraceful stepmother only cares to go to parties. Every day I have to listen to the same thing, 'Cinderella do whatever you're sisters tell you to do and make sure that the house is clean. If anything goes wrong, then you're in big, big, big trouble!'

I want to go to the ball so I can meet the prince, but my sisters and my mother won't let me because they want me to do all the work while they go to the ball and have the time of their lives. Please do something to get me out of this hell. I hope to hear from you soon.

Yours faithfully,
Cinderella.

Humaira Chowdhury (10)
Palfrey Junior School, Walsall

Dear Agony Fairy

Dear Agony Fairy,

I am writing this letter because everybody ignores me. First of all my dad doesn't like me, he only likes those two dumbos, Amy and Sally, my two stepsisters. The prince didn't invite me to his palace disco, however, he invited the two dumbos, because they are goody-two-shoes, well I'm not!

Everybody calls me 'Sinful Cinderella' just because I break things and steal stuff and other wonderful things. I do it because I have nothing better to do and if they don't like me, why should I like them? Anyway what's so bad about that? Do you think I'm sinful or horrible? I want to go to the palace disco and have a good pair of jeans, with a sparkly top and a pair of high heels.

So can you give me a spell that will make me, what's the word - oh yeah - good? Tell the truth, do you think I have good manners? Because they are *so* boring, my stepmum and dad always brag that I should get some. Everybody thinks I'm rude, do you think I'm rude? Well I think I'm not rude, I try my best not to be.

Just do your advising rubbish and reply soon, I can't wait, OK!

Yours sincerely,

Cinderella.

Naeema Goni (10)
Palfrey Junior School, Walsall

Puss In Boots

Dear Your Majesty,

Today I saw an extraordinary cat wearing boots! The feline talked to an unusual boy. This cat told the boy where some gold was hidden.

Your Majesty, if we ask this outstanding feline where more gold is, maybe it will answer. This will mean victory for us and it will make us very rich. The other thing is that they are going to kill you!

As I am your adviser, I say that you should capture this cat and it should be kept out of your way. You should also ask it where the gold is. Please make up your mind soon or the weird cat will strike!

Yours sincerely,
Waqar Syed (Adviser).

Waqar Syed (10)
Palfrey Junior School, Walsall

The Three Bossy Bears

The three bossy bears had woken up, they went downstairs one by one. They sat down and small bossy said, 'I want some porridge,' and Mummy bossy said, 'No because you've had some already.'

Daddy bossy said, angrily, 'Let's go outside,' so they went. They met Goldifox and the three bossy bears said, 'Look there's a good fox,' and they started to cheek her.

Goldifox started to cry and she went home and told her parents and her parents said, 'If they do it again, we will sort them out,' so Goldifox went to the forest to get some flowers.

Goldifox met the three bossy bears who said, 'Were you crying yesterday?'

Goldifox said, 'If you cheek me, my dad will sort you out.'

The three bossy bears said, 'We're not scared of your dad.'

So Goldifox went home and told her dad and her dad said, 'Twice you have made my daughter cry so please can you say sorry?'

They said sorry.

After that they said bye to each other and they went home.

Every time the three bossy bears went to the forest and Goldifox was there, the three bears would give a present to Goldifox and Goldifox would say thank you, so Goldifox changed the three bossy bears' names to the three kind bears and they lived happily ever after.

Halima Begum
Palfrey Junior School, Walsall

Aneliese The Mermaid And The Dangerous Shark

One day Aneliese's mother told Aneliese to give her granny some buns because she was ill so she set off. On the way, when Aneliese was swimming, she saw a beautiful, shiny, astonishing silver shell. Aneliese picked it up. Just then she heard a voice. 'What's your name?' the voice said again.

'Who's there?' replied Aneliese.

Just then *out of nowhere!* There appeared a shark. 'Where are you going?' the shark said in a kind, sweet, polite voice.

'I'm, I'm ... going to my granny's to give her some buns because she is ill,' said Aneliese.

'Where does she live?' the shark shouted out aloud.

'5th cave on the right.'

The shark knew a short cut, then the shark had an idea. If he could hide her gran somewhere.

The shark arrived at her gran's house. The shark said, 'Can I come in?'

'Yes,' replied her gran. The shark came in and hid Aneliese's gran behind a long green seaweed and tied her up. The shark came inside and put Granny's glasses and clothes on.

Just then Aneliese came in. 'What big eyes you have,' she said surprisingly after she'd put the basket down.

'All the better to see you with?'

'What big teeth you have.'

'All the better to eat you with.' *Jump!* The shark swam out of bed to eat Aneliese.

She screamed as she swam.

Rupert the dolphin and his friend were passing by. They swam around him until he got tired. Then Aneliese just told them what had happened. They found her gran and lived happily ever after.

Tahmina Ahmed (9)
Palfrey Junior School, Walsall

How Cinderella Became Rich

One day, there was a girl named Cinders, that wasn't her real name, her real name was Cinderella. She had brown hair and brown eyes, she lived with her parents in an old rusty cottage. They were really poor.

One sunny morning, Cinderella was sitting by the old window, she was looking at the beautiful nature around her. However, suddenly, out of nowhere appeared some pigs, so she went to see them.

Several minutes later, Cinderella said to the pigs, 'What are you doing here?' Then they replied, 'We're lost!'

'I'll help you,' said Cinderella. Then she said, 'Let's go.'

On the way Cinderella saw a tall beanstalk so they climbed up it. Suddenly a monster came and grabbed them and locked them up. She was flabbergasted, her body was shaking like a washing machine.

After a while, the monster came and said to Cinderella, 'Marry me!'

'No!' replied Cinderella, then she ran and took a bag of gold and gave it to her parents and they became rich. Then they lived happily ever after (except for the pigs who were eaten by the monster).

Rahima Begum Malik (10)
Palfrey Junior School, Walsall

The Bad Girl Cinderella

Once upon a time there was a girl called Cinderella, who was a mean and a dreadful little girl, she had two lovely sisters who were kind, they also taught her manners.

The problem was that Cinderella thought that she was prettier than everyone else. Then Cinderella and the two lovely sisters kept arguing about whom was going to marry the handsome prince. Also Cindy kept crying and whatever she thought was right was what she did.

Suddenly the handsome prince entered with the shiny glass slipper. First it was the two lovely sisters' turns. The sisters tried the glass slipper. Really it never fitted them but they were squeezing it, then the handsome prince got fed up and cut the two lovely sisters' heads off. Cinderella got very scared, she decided to not have a turn because she wanted to marry someone else.

Cinderella was thinking, thinking about her future. Who should she marry? She had an idea, the idea was that she married the jam maker, the jam maker liked her too, they were a smart couple.

Finally she kissed the jam maker and went to the ball, dancing and singing, having an amusing time and they lived happily ever after.

Sharmin Khatun (10)
Palfrey Junior School, Walsall

The Three Juicy Pigs
And The Manipulating Wolf

There was once a manipulating wolf, who fancied some nice juicy pigs and thought to himself, *shall I eat them with figs?* But as we all know the manipulating wolf was also very clever and had decided to write a poster and stick it all around the town centre.

So as a result this is what he wrote:
'Hi little juicy pigs!
I would like to eat you with figs,
And a drink of orange juice,
Plus for my dessert, chocolate mousse.
Would you please come,
It will be so much fun,
I shall give you anything I like,
Especially a sharp pointy bite,
My mouth is starting to water,
More than a pint and a quarter,
And I'll gobble you in a *blink, blink* of an eye,
But please don't be shy'.

Marriyah Hussain (10)
Palfrey Junior School, Walsall

Cinderella - My Sad Life

Long, long ago I lived with two outrageous sisters, one called Janah and one called Hannah. They both were dominating. My dad married their mum, she was so horrible, she kicked me up the bum and made me do all the work. My life was horrible. All I did was work, wash, cook and clean. I had no fun, like a young girl should.

One terrific night there was a letter on the doorstep. I was busy making dinner so my sisters grabbed it and tore it open. It said:

'You beautiful ladies,
Come to the ball,
Just for you
In a gorgeous hall'.

My stepmother and sisters decided to go but I had to stay and scrub the toilets. I was just getting under the rim, when I saw a blinding flash of light. It was my fairy godmother. With just one wave of her wand, I had everything I needed to attend the ball.

As I stood shimmering in my fine dress, the prince requested a dance with me. We swirled around the floor all night, he told me I was the one.

So did I become queen? Did I have a diamond tiara and go on foreign trips? No! He didn't want a wife. He wanted a cleaner for the palace kitchens, so here I am up to my elbows in Fairy Liquid, passing the dishes to my fairy godmother, who's drying up.

Nafisah Khatoon (10)
Palfrey Junior School, Walsall

Jack And The Beanstalk

One day Jack's mother told him to sell their cow at the supermarket. So off he went. On the way he met a strange old man who said, 'Can I have this cow for this magic bean?'

Jack went home and told his mum that he'd seen an old man, he'd given him the cow and in return got a magic bean. Jack's mother got very angry and snatched the magic bean, then she threw the magic bean outside, in the disgusting garden of theirs as she was so cross. His mother got a vacuum cleaner and smacked him with it.

In the night, the magic bean began to grow, it grew and grew and strange fruit began to appear.

The next morning, when Jack woke up, he peered through his window and there before his eyes was a baked bean tree. Tins of lovely beans in tomatoey sauce hung down between the leaves.

Jack picked all the tins and sold them. More grew back, so he sold them too, after a year Jack was one of the richest men in the world and had an enormous mansion and three helicopters. But even to this day, he makes his mother do all the cleaning because of the time she smacked him with the vacuum cleaner.

Akif Ahmed (10)
Palfrey Junior School, Walsall

One Rainy Day

One rainy day there was once two boys and two girls, their names were Steve, Ruby, Connor and Lucy, Ruby was the cleverest out of all of them. Ruby liked school and always liked everything. One day she asked her teacher, 'Can I have more homework and my friends?'

The teacher said, 'Oh yes, of course you can but if you don't finish you will get detention!'

After the weekend Ruby forgot about the homework and told her teacher, 'Sir, I forgot my homework!'

'You and your friends are having detention after school!'

After school they had detention, Steve shouted, 'Open the door!'

Ruby said, 'It's jammed, there's nothing you can do!'

Lucy screamed, 'There's a fire and it's coming here!'

Steve tried to open the door but the fire was getting closer, they all pushed and pushed the door, it opened a little bit but it was no good until a bit more opened and Connor said, 'Come on, it's nearly opening.'

'We can do it if we just use our strength.'

They all pushed as hard as they could and it finally opened.

All they had to do was get a fire extinguisher and get out.

Finally the teacher came and helped, and they all came out but the school had to close to get the school repaired.

They all lived happily ever after.

Sumaya Tuki (8)
St Andrew's School, Birmingham

There Was Once ...

There was once four children who are actually the heroes of this story.

Their names were Noha, Paige, Isha and Patricia. They were in class 3CA and they were sitting quietly doing an assessment. If they made one sound, their strict teacher Miss Ashford would shout at them.

'This is boring,' whispered Patricia.

'Quiet!' shouted Miss Ashford.

Suddenly the Head came in with bad news. The Head said, 'Sorry children, there's a flood in the school and we are marooned here for a month, and no hot dinners.'

The children all groaned. They all sulked when it was dinnertime.

When they were eating, they heard a whooshing noise. They knew what it was straight away. They told everyone in the hall to hold onto their legs, they asked why. Noha said, 'There's a flood coming in here.'

When the flood came, they were ready, they kicked their legs like crazy and got to safety. They never got marooned in the school again.

Nona Said
St Andrew's School, Birmingham

The Pied Piper Of Hamelin 2

The mayor stood with his mouth wide open, and the council stood and watched really still. They watched, still frozen like ice, the children happily ran by, they could only follow with their eyes. The crowd shouted behind the piper's back, when all the children reached the mountainside, a magnificent hole opened very wide.

The Pied Piper went in and the children followed, then when they were inside to the last child, the doors in the mountainside closed very fast. I never said last child did I? No! I never! One was really lame so he could not run all of the way. They reached the hole finding it empty.

Isha Sikander (8)
St Andrew's School, Birmingham

The Adventures Of The Super Gang

The Super Gang are having a fantastic break from their work until a ship which looks like a piece of hell is lurking around and is set to destroy ...

The ship is getting closer and the bombs are demolishing the city, they zoom down as fast as bullets. When the Super Gang heard of this, they very quickly change into their uniforms. Flame and Pryo have fireproof costumes which are as bright as the sun; Muscle Man has green shorts and the rest have bright green and orange costumes.

Squirt! Aqua Man throws a water ball as big and wet as a whale but it cannot bring the ship down so Elastico stretches up and drags the ship down to the ground. Muscle Man smashes the ship open - finally they can get in.

They open a hatch and see a round piece of metal which looks like a heart, they realise the ship is alive! But before they can blink the ship takes off! It takes them to the moon and all of their fellow superheroes are all trapped. Before the ship can take off without them, they all jump in. A sign flashing with red says *Self Destruct.*

Joshua Claridge (9)
St Joseph's RC Junior School, Nuneaton

The Land Of Golden Pears

Once, there were three friends, Elissa, Haley and Abily strolling along the winding path, but a few minutes later, *zap!* They were gone. About half an hour later, they reappeared but they were not on the winding path, they were in the Land of Golden Pears.

When they arrived at the front gates, (they were as big as a giant's boulder) they were engraved with the words: *The Land Of Golden Pears*.

There was a little man sitting on a stool called Bob guarding the land. Bob had beautiful golden hair which was down to his ears; eyes which were as blue as the flowing river and he was so small he was nearly a dwarf! The three friends asked if he wanted to be their friend and so Bob agreed but only if they helped him guard the land, so they did.

One day they were having a picnic in the beautiful daylight of the land, which smelt like fresh fruit smoothies, when Lily the burglar came sneaking in and stole *all* of the pears! When they strolled back to the gates, they saw that all the pears had gone! The three girls questioned Bob about what was going to happen and he told them that the trees may not survive and they needed a plan. Soon they thought of one, to go and find her.

The next day, they set off, and after a long march down the dusty path, they spotted her in her big log house that had a blazing fire in, which crackled like fireworks. Bob asked her to give the apples back but instead she ran off, so Bob ran up the path trying to catch her. They ran around until Lily ran out of breath and she stopped. Bob took the apples and told her never to do that again, so she didn't, but Bob didn't know if the trees would survive. Nobody knew …

Haley Webb (9)
St Joseph's RC Junior School, Nuneaton

The Flying Scot

'John, it's time to go,' Mum called as John sprinted downstairs and into the car. Today it was John's birthday so he was going to his grandad's house for dinner. When he arrived Grandad sat him down and gave him a large parcel wrapped in ruby-red wrapping paper. When John opened it, his face exploded with surprise. 'A Scalectrix!' he shouted.

After dinner, John went exploring. Suddenly he heard a miaow - it was Scabbers - John suddenly spotted a hockey stick in the corner of his eye - it was electric-blue and sprayed in gold, were the words 'X 4000'. 'I knew that you would like that.' John spun round - it was his grandad. 'You can have it if you want.'

John went home and set up his Scalectrix. Him and his dad played for hours, until it was time for bed.

The next day John got up and prepared himself for the hockey club. He had decided to use Grandad's hockey stick. As Mum drove him to the hockey club, he felt a tingle inside his hands, it was the hockey stick but John ignored it. When they arrived, the hockey stick had changed colour from blue to red and back again. John knew the stick was special. Mark the coach shouted, 'Four laps of the pitch, move it!' Suddenly John was ahead of everyone. When he completed the laps his coach said, 'Listen up! These are the people who are in the team - Morgan, James, Luke, John and Jacob.'

John couldn't believe it. After club, John and his mum went to the chippy, 'I'm so proud,' his mum said.

Two weeks later and it was time for the big game. A few bumps and bruises and the game was finished with the score of 4-1. That meant John's team were through to the finals. The next match came extremely quickly but John did not realise that someone had switched his hockey stick with a decoy. In the first half, John's team were losing 1-0. In the second half thanks to a fantastic goal from Morgan, they were drawing 1-1. In the last 2 minutes John was in possession of the puck and with a blinding shot, he scored. The match was over.

After the presentation, everyone went for a special dinner, but he never found his stick ever again.

Harry Bennett (9)
St Joseph's RC Junior School, Nuneaton

The Jewellery Box

It was a wet, rainy day in the village of Oakwood. The raindrops were as big as whales and suddenly ... *splish, splash, splosh!*

Leah was in her bedroom playing with her dolls until she heard some faint noises, they were coming from her jewellery box. She tiptoed over to it as it was smiling at her. The box stood on a stand, next to her bed and Leah sat down to open it. *Silence!*

The box was decorated with painted patterns, purple beads like beautiful beetles and red rubies like a rooster crowing at dawn. Finally a carved wooden butterfly.

Suddenly ... the box slowly opened and it was gleaming pure white. Leah was nowhere to be seen, she must have vanished!

Leah was whooshing down, down, down into nothingness. She found herself on a phoenix; Leah asked the phoenix where she was and felt a bit puzzled. The phoenix was called Rose and explained that they were in the Land of ... *Autumn!* The Land of Autumn was as golden as a petal falling from a daffodil. *But* it was cursed by an evil wizard that came from the Land of *Winter* who tried to *freeze* everything.

Rose bombarded down to a giant sunflower with two dragons wandering around it, there was a blue dragon called Sky and a green dragon called Emerald. If you touched the sunflower and made a wish, it would come true, so that is what Leah did. She touched the sunflower and wished she was home again. In a second or two she opened her eyes and she was playing with her dolls again. Leah yelled, 'I'm home!' or at least she thought she was. She spied the ruby-red plumage of the phoenix in the corner of her eye.

Lily Lee (9)
St Joseph's RC Junior School, Nuneaton

Graveyard Of Ghouls!

Jason was a tall, generous boy with eyes that were shinier than the twinkling stars. Jason had a friend named Mary, she had eyes as blue as sapphires, she also had hair like a raven's coat.

Jason and Mary were chatting when suddenly they felt a rush of wind that bolted through their hair, they stopped still and observed a graveyard. The sky was as dark as ebony.

Jason and Mary crept into the graveyard as silent as mice. They found a strange tombstone that said *Do Not Touch Or Beware!* Jason confidently touched it and both Mary and Jason fell into a mysterious hole.

They both bombarded down into the hole with a *crash!* Then silence. Mary crept silently into the murky cavern that only had one door; Jason was trying to open the encrypted, dirty door but he failed. Mary was watching and she accidentally triggered a button that opened the wall.

Jason stepped silently into the room. Mary followed. They both identified some coffins which were as black as nothingness. The door slammed shut. *Bang!* The coffin lids slid open and ghouls appeared. Jason and Mary ran as fast as cheetahs away from the ghouls, they were right behind them. The ghouls had eyes as red as blood. Would Mary and Jason escape or be captured ... ?

Stephen Snounou (9)
St Joseph's RC Junior School, Nuneaton

Factory Of Dreams

On a blazing morning, the birds were singing like a choir of angels and the sun was as bright as the North Star's beam.

It's about to become a dream come true for Liam, Ben, Stephen and Jordan. They were about to enter the factory of dreams. They were decorated with smiles as big watermelons.

As soon as they were in, the colours shone like a tear from an angel's eye and as bright as a rainbow.

Meanwhile Ben was looking at a machine that said: *'Do not touch!'* So Ben jumped in and turned into a chocolate monkey. Everybody started to search but he was melting really quickly and *pop!* The others were coated in melted fudge chocolate, was that Ben?

Liam Hutchinson (9)
St Joseph's RC Junior School, Nuneaton

The Magic Flower

There was once a little girl called Lily and she was new to the neighbourhood. She had hair as soft as silk and eyes as blue as the azure sky.

She lived near to the forest and she was told by her friend that it was magic. Lily did not believe her so when she had settled in, she went to investigate. When she took one little step in, she saw dancing elves in little green suits. She also saw flowers swaying in the breeze, they were humming a welcome song of joy, but one particular flower was not only a different colour, it was not singing! Lily strolled to it and touched the flower with her soft hand and the whole forest shone as bright as the twinkling sun.

Zap!

It transported Lily to a magic forest! There were twinkling waterfalls that little fairies were sliding down like a polar bear on an iceberg. Lily could not believe her eyes. There were busy bees collecting their harvest; leaping frogs jumping from one lily pad to another, it was a dream come true. There was blossom as pink as roses, but best of all, a bright sun that looked like a golden penny floating in the air, hovering like a spider in his web.

An elf twice as small as her came over and asked if Lily would help him find the thief of gold, so that minute she again touched the flower which brought her to the land, and she found the thief! He was wearing a waistcoat and he still had the gold in his pocket. She emptied his pockets of every last piece of gold and gave it back to the elf.

The whole of the land gave her a party - it was wonderful! There were frilly tablecloths coating long tables; they released sapphire butterflies and there were bunny rabbits hopping around. But where was the thief ... ?

Olivia McAlinden (8)
St Joseph's RC Junior School, Nuneaton

Magic Theme Park

James is a young, polite boy and he has blue eyes that twinkle in the golden sun. One day James' family, the Hamptons, went to the ancient plant shop and as they strolled round the enormous shop James found a pamphlet. It said: 'Magic Theme Park, (Only in Glasgow!)'.

James treasured the pamphlet like it was a pot of gold and asked his friends Hannah and Lee if they wanted to go. Hannah had long, shiny ginger hair that smelt like coconuts. On the other hand, Lee wore glasses and he had green eyes that looked like the grass in a beautiful rainforest. James' dad, Paul, took them to the park and left them there.

As they scampered into the park like cheetahs, Lee dragged James and Hannah to the Power Tower (a tall tower that drops you face first down a 150 metre tower). They crawled onto the seats, they started to rise. Hannah wanted to get off but it was too late. They had already reached the top and then *whoosh! 'Argh!'* cried Lee.

'Help!' shouted James and then it was all over.

After the shocking ride on the Power Tower, Lee suggested they should stop in the magic fish bar.

James shouted, 'But we have *no* money!'

'Oh, I have,' replied Hannah. So they all stopped and ate fish and chips covered with ketchup. Hannah pushed Lee and James to the Magic Wonderland but Lee and James refused to ride so Hannah went on by herself but when Hannah's train came out, she had disappeared, into thin air, just like when you rub out a word, *gone forever.*

Suddenly Lee spotted Hannah being dragged into the sky by a bear shouting, 'I'm taking you to the animal kingdom!' When Hannah arrived, the blue bear showed her all the other bears and then he took her to a chocolate factory and left her there.

All of a sudden something was fluttering down like a dove. Lee shouted, 'It's Hannah.'

James replied, 'Or is it ...?'

Jacob Goddard (9)
St Joseph's RC Junior School, Nuneaton

The Haunted House

The door makes a creaky sound. A rat scurries across the floorboards that are creaky as I creep across them. The staircase is as brown as mud and a spider makes a cobweb in the corner of the room. I shuffle up the staircase, then I hear a *bang!* Then silence! Was it a ghost?

The moon glows as I walk past the dusty cobwebbed window. It smells like burnt ashes while the rain tiptoes on the pond outside. Ants scurry on the bookcase because the room had not been cleaned for years.

Something touches my back, what is it? I turn around to peer at what touched me, but when I turn around the apparition has vanished! I hear footsteps coming towards the house, it could be the people who lived here, and died here.

The spiders are making a crown of cobwebs on my head. It is as dark as a cave with not even a little flickering flame of light. Then I go outside - there is a graveyard; it is haunting me a lot.

There is a layer of frosty dust tickling the top of the pond. The trees sway in the vicious wind while the grass is scraping my knees as I walk. My heart is beating like a drum. I can hear something running behind me. What is it? Will it harm me? I turn around and I see a werewolf bearing its white pearly teeth at me. I start to run, it's chasing me. It has grey fur like a cloud in the rainy sky and eyes as bright as the fires of Hell ... 'Argh!'

Elle Simpson (9)
St Joseph's RC Junior School, Nuneaton

The Magic Car

Rose had got a new car for her birthday that had flowers on that were as red as freshly picked cherries. She travelled everywhere in it but soon she found a button that did something special, very special. She pressed that button many times and the car glowed like a bright torch.

The next day she was driving to work and suddenly, just as she was going to turn on the radio, her golden hair swung round like a roundabout and before she knew it, she was in Mexico! Her heart was beating like a drum so, she climbed back into her car, that had just turned orange!

She was hungry, she had nothing to eat. As she was driving, she pressed the button again and the same thing happened but this time she was back in her cosy home, but just as she jumped out, she was off again. Now she was whizzing all around the world like a fly. Soon the car stopped and she was on the moon. Silence. She was petrified. She sat in the car because she couldn't stay any longer.

Suddenly she started spinning again and she ended up at home. Was it just a dream? She took the car to the dump as quick as lightning and, just as she walked away, she saw the car spin and disappear.

Marina Davidson (8)
St Joseph's RC Junior School, Nuneaton

The Family Of Cats

Long ago, in a far-off land, there lived a family of cats, a mum, a dad and a baby. They all sat there as bored as bored can be, in their cosy home. All they wanted was to play with any toy at all. But they were all terrified of the monster named 'The River Lizard' who guarded all of their toys.

One day the kitten decided to go to play with his toys. Suddenly the terrifying monster jumped out. 'Who dares play with my toys? I will bake you for my breakfast.'

'But I'm only a kitten, why don't you wait for my mum? I wouldn't fill you up a tiny bit.' Then the monster wanted a meatier cat.

Later on the mummy cat came to play with her toys, but the terrifying monster jumped out, 'Who dares play with my toys? I will cook you for my lunch.'

But the mummy cat intelligently replied, 'But I am only a normal-sized cat, I wouldn't fill you up a tiny bit. Why don't you wait for my husband? He is much bigger and fatter, he would fill you up much more.'

After that the dad cat came out but then the terrifying monster jumped out. 'Who dares play with my toys? I will eat you for my evening snack.'

'Oh no you won't, because I have the sharpest claws!' The dad scratched the monster and he ran away. Now the family can play with their toys whenever they want to.

Franklin Davies (7)
St Joseph's RC Junior School, Nuneaton

The Robin Hood Letter

Dear Snow White,

My name is Robin Hood and I am being bullied by seven dwarves. Could you give me some advice on how to stop them because they keep on calling me names. I get wound up, when all I want is to make friends. So please can you help me? I really would like new friends.

Yours truly,
Robin Hood.

Curtis Simmonds (9)
St Mary's Immaculate Catholic Primary School, Warwick

Dear Agony Aunt

Dear Agony Aunt,

I have a problem, yesterday a girl came into my cottage and she ate all my porridge. I was very angry! Then I went in the living room because I wanted to sit down. I saw Mummy's and Daddy's chair, but not mine! I just saw lots of wooden pieces on the floor. They were from my chair, someone had broken it.

I was so tired I went upstairs. I found a girl asleep in *my bed*! So I got my mummy and daddy to scare her off, so I could go to sleep.

How do I stop her from coming back?

Please help!

Love from Baby Bear.

Zoe Bench (11)
St Mary's Immaculate Catholic Primary School, Warwick

The Ring Of The Ancients

'This ring was given to me by my mum and now I'm giving it to you. Be careful with it.' My mum was the kind of mum that's overprotective more than usual, after all, she is a witch.

I'm Amy, I actually can't believe I'm a witch, I mean, witches are weird, this is a true story. True to me, true to my brother. Here it is, in brief.

My brother got himself trapped in my ring because he was looking through the spell book (I could never trust him with anything!) 'It's his fault!' I told my mum but *nnoooo* she just loves my brother even though he's an annoying little brat!

So when I told her she looked in the spell book and said, 'The only way you can free him is by having faith in the person who's trapped.' So I started to believe in my brother and all his abilities. I tried every day to think of things I liked about him. A few months later, it worked, but I think that might have been because of the crying I did. I learnt an important thing, I actually missed my brother.

Anoosha Babu (11)
St Mary's Immaculate Catholic Primary School, Warwick

Mini Saga

I feel myself go red as I write my work down on paper, I try too hard, which puts me off
   so much. I don't know why I am so scared; I don't know why I am so worried. Now look how good this piece of writing is.

Ross Chamberlain (10)
St Mary's Immaculate Catholic Primary School, Warwick

Evacuation Of The Irish

'Good afternoon to all the people out there. I would just like to say good afternoon! Oh, sorry did I just repeat myself? Well, anyway let's introduce this song, Kaiser Chiefs - I Predict A Riot!' John Foster reported into the microphone as Emily and Louise were chatting away about that night's episode of EastEnders! Then, *beep, beep, beep!* An email had been sent through the computer all the way from Cork! It read: *'This is an emergency, there has been an overflow of the River Shannon and we need to contact all of the population through anyway we can. Obviously some people will be driving, so it would be a great help if you could tell everyone listening to their local radio the bad news. Thank you. Deepside Council.'*

When John got this message, he turned the music off as quickly as he could and Matthew said worriedly, 'Hello I'm sorry to interrupt your enjoyment of the Kaiser Chiefs but I have an important announcement.'

He ruffled the piece of paper with the email on and told them the bad news. 'I'm sorry guys but you will have to make your way down to Belfast airport as soon as possible, but don't speed or race, drive carefully.'

Meanwhile Jake Warford was right next to Belfast airport and pulled in. He met lots of other people there and tried to calm them down.

However the River Shannon was still overflowing and not everyone knew about it.

Dannielle Hover (10)
St Mary's Immaculate Catholic Primary School, Warwick

Dear Agony Aunt

Dear Agony Aunt,

I am writing to tell you about Goldilocks. She will not be friends with me, I have to say sorry for my dad scaring her. I have asked her if we could have a talk, bought her chocolates and flowers, even invited her back to my house.

Oh please help!

Write back as soon as possible.

Yours sincerely,

Baby Bear.

Samuel Slemensek (10)
St Mary's Immaculate Catholic Primary School, Warwick

My Birthday

The house door opened for me. Slowly, I walked in, I was shaking. I heard voices, but no one was there. Suddenly I felt someone tap me, but still I could see no one. I took off my glasses and cleaned them.

Surprise! I had forgotten it's my birthday!

Yasmin Feasey (9)
St Mary's Immaculate Catholic Primary School, Warwick

Dear Mr Wizard

Dear Mr Wizard,

Can you help me to be friends with the Three Billy Goats Gruff? Last week they were walking across my bridge, I popped up to say hello, but they ran for their lives. I'm just too big and scary. What should I do?

Yours truly,
Mr Troll.

Luke Smith (10)
St Mary's Immaculate Catholic Primary School, Warwick

Letter To Big Bad Wolf

Dear Big Bad Wolf,

Please can you help me? I am getting bullied at school, I told my teacher Miss Cinderella, but she won't listen. Can you teach them a lesson for me?

Yours truly,
Master Piglet.

Alexander Pilkington (10)
St Mary's Immaculate Catholic Primary School, Warwick

Dear Ugly Sisters

Dear Ugly Sisters,

On behalf of the Council, we are writing to you, the Ugly Sisters, about your jealousy. We know you wanted to marry the prince but the slipper did not fit either of you, so he married Cinderella.

Please do not be jealous.

Yours sincerely,

The Council.

Blake Wareing (10)
St Mary's Immaculate Catholic Primary School, Warwick

Witch's Spell

Eye of piranha, a baby's nappy,
Make it quick, make it snappy,
Leg of horse, feathers of a hawk,
I'll use the hawk instead of pork.

There will be no hero,
Just a plain zero,
Alligator's teeth,
Which will cut off her feet,
Will Snow White survive?
Oh I will thrive.

Cut her hair,
Make it bare,
Throw down the tower,
Let me have the power,
I see her cower,
Because she ain't got no power.

Scrunch up her face,
Make it a disgrace,
Cut off her legs,
Unless she begs,
Will Rapunzel be about,
When I take her out?

Khalid Saeed (11)
Somerville Primary School, Birmingham

Da Witch's Spell

Revolting hairy armpits and some fresh worms from the lawn,
And a ballistic taxi driver that always blows his horn,
A bling-bling T-shirt that's dazzling white,
And then a dead person's heart who always caused a fight.

Bogeys from Pinocchio's nose,
And toenails from an African man's toes,
Sweat from Zidane,
And moves from Jackie Chan.

This is how I'll make my wormy-haired, hairy armpits,
Fight causing martial arts scarecrow,
Which at being mad is a pro,
With toenails as big as a bow.

This recipe is intended for teenagers who are measly,
Just like Harry Potter's own Ron Weasley,
Hopefully they'll all be terrified,
Or down the drain will go my pride.

Suhail Chaudhry (11)
Somerville Primary School, Birmingham

Dear Fairy Godmother

181 Witch's Street
Fairy Lane
High Palace
B94 4EN

6th July 2006

Dear Fairy Godmother,

My name is Rapunzel and I need your assistance desperately. I am trapped in a tower, I am surrounded by 4 dusty and solid walls. I really want to have trustworthy friends but I am a prisoner in this deserted tower. I tried exclaiming once so someone can come and eliminate me. I always get the witch's wrath.

I've got a huge complication at the moment so have you any suggestions, you can help me with? The witch has an evil laugh. I don't know what her next cunning plan is or what will happen to me. *Please* can you think of something quick?

If I take a slight glimpse out of the window, I can spot ecstatic children playing, I wish I could do that but I've lost my childhood already being locked up in high tower as a prisoner. I miss my family so could you do something to send me back to my lovely home?

If you have anything that could help me, please could you write and tell me, I would be most grateful.

Yours truly,
Rapunzel.

Sonia Khanum (11)
Somerville Primary School, Birmingham

Mini Saga

My body is shaking and my teeth are chattering. I feel as if there is a ghost behind me. My neck is sweating. It is really creepy, there is no room, I feel squashed. My mouth is wide and I am very scared. I light the candle and work.

Shweb Uddin (9)
Somerville Primary School, Birmingham

The Graveyard

I was walking along the dusty old path when I felt very exhausted. I sat in the middle of the graveyard when a spooky sound appeared right next to me, I was looking around, but there was no one there.

I felt as though I was going to drop down …

Zakia Kalsoom (9)
Somerville Primary School, Birmingham

Graveyard

I was walking out of the shops at 9pm. I was walking when suddenly I walked past a *graveyard*. There was a howling voice, it was all gloomy and it turned darker than before, I was scared stiff. Behind me was a tap, I was scared. 'Mum!' I shouted.

Kanwal Hassan (9)
Somerville Primary School, Birmingham

In The Dark, Spooky Attic

In the attic, my heart beat like a drum and I was shivering like I was cold. Suddenly I heard the door make a noise, I said, 'Who's there?' But it was no one. Then I looked up and I saw bats flying as fast as cats.

    I ran, fast!

Umair Badshah (9)
Somerville Primary School, Birmingham

The Floating Lady

There I was, passing the graveyard, suddenly I stopped. I was shaking, I was sweating. I went in the graveyard, I knew I wasn't scared. I was nearly at the end when suddenly I saw a lady floating in the air. She disappeared, I ran home and didn't tell anyone.

Sabera Begum (9)
Somerville Primary School, Birmingham

Alone In The Attic

When I came back home, I went up to the attic to get my toy, then I felt that I'd been locked in. I tried to look for a torch, then I heard a voice and something falling.

The voice, 'I've got your torch and I am a ghost.'

Wasim Mehmood (9)
Somerville Primary School, Birmingham

In The Spooky Attic

In the attic my heart beat like a football and I was shivering as if I were in the Antarctic.

Suddenly, I heard the door open like an open mouth of an ugly giant. I was sweating like I'd finished playing a football match. I ran fast out of the door.

Irfhan Khan (9)
Somerville Primary School, Birmingham

Mini Saga

I heard a noise. My feet wobbled like jelly, my face was sweaty and my tummy was grumbling. My ankle twisted and my shoulder shook. It was creepy and dark.

I was frightened, I looked up and saw the blue sky. I had found the way out of the forest.

Zainab Jabeen (9)
Somerville Primary School, Birmingham

Mini Saga

My tummy lurches, it rocks left and right. I get dizzy, I feel like I am going to vomit. I get sweaty palms. Sweat runs down my neck, I feel like I cannot breathe.

Once I get on dry land I wonder why I'm so scared of boats.

Yasar Javed (9)
Somerville Primary School, Birmingham

Mini Saga

I look down, everybody looks like ants, my heart pounds. My palms sweat. My lips and throat are dry, my body feels stiff. Why did I have to stand on this high wall?

My feet sweat, I close my eyes and take a deep breath, and jump down very bravely.

Zakia Amer (9)
Somerville Primary School, Birmingham

Mini Saga

I can sense animals like wolves approaching closer to me. I see darkness and trees everywhere. My throat is dry, my pulse is racing and my heartbeat pounding. No one knows where I am.

As I walk, I see a path leading towards a straight road.

Ariba Afzal (9)
Somerville Primary School, Birmingham

Night Light!

Mrs Goody was a little old lady who lived in a little white house. She had three pets, a cat, a dog and a bird. When Mrs Goody went to sleep, her three pets did too. When Mrs Goody got up, her pets did too.

It was a hot night and Mrs Goody couldn't sleep. *Some cold water would be good*, she thought. Mrs Goody got up and put on the light, 'It's morning!'

The bird sang. 'It's not morning,' said Mrs Goody, 'go back to sleep,' but the bird didn't go back to sleep and it sang and sang.

The cat woke up, 'Good morning,' he said in a sleepy way. The dog woke up too and thought it was morning too.

Soon all the animals in the street thought it was morning so they made lots of noise, then all the people in the street woke up. Finally the man from down the street came. He was a policeman, he went to Mrs Goody's house and said, 'What's happened?'

Mrs Goody replied and said, 'I was hot so I put the light on to have some water!'

'Stop!' said the policeman and he started to laugh.

'Turn off the light,' he said. Then Mrs Goody started to laugh too, so she turned off the light and everybody went back to sleep.

Nosheba Shafiq (10)
Somerville Primary School, Birmingham

Stuck In The Toilet

I ran to the girls' toilets, I was desperate, I bolted the door - I put the lock on. When I had finished, I tried to unlock the door. I had locked the door but it was stuck. I shouted, 'Help!' Someone came, they kicked the door off, *phew!*

Alina Choudry (9)
Somerville Primary School, Birmingham

Mini Saga

Darkness all around me, it is creepy and spooky. I feel the shiver in my body and veins. I feel something under my bed. I hear the creepy and spooky sound all around me. It is making me scared. What was that? What could it be? A ghost!

Salina Mahmood (9)
Somerville Primary School, Birmingham

The Doll Killer!

Deep through the trees stood a haunted mansion. It stood near a graveyard. In the mansion lived a new family, the Smiths. One hazy night the Smiths were celebrating. It was little Ella's birthday. They had a magnificent time. After a while Ella's parents gave her a special doll for her birthday. Ella was so thrilled that she didn't go to sleep.

While she was in bed, she heard her door slam and all of a sudden she heard her parents scream, she slowly and quietly went down the stairs and she fell in tears, there, lying on the floor were her parents covered in blood.

She was so infuriated that she started to scream, she fell to her knees and wept. She heard the door slam again, she turned around in anger and suddenly, something leapt on her and in surprise, she fell on the cold ground. The room was in silence, there, stood covered in blood was the doll that her parents bought her for her birthday, it was holding two sharp knives.

In the morning, an old man had seen them lying dead, he called the police and they took them away. They banned anyone from going to the mansion. Now the doll is out there, watch out, don't let it come round her house!

Khalida Begum (10)
Somerville Primary School, Birmingham

In The Cupboard

I was in my room when I head a noise, then I heard it again. It was a noise you would never hear, a type of howl and it was coming from the cupboard.

Suddenly I rushed to the cupboard and flung it open. There in the middle was a huge, ugly green monster. I punched it but my hand went straight through his bulgy body, then I had an idea.

I got a bottle of shampoo and squirted it at him, he melted into a mixture of yellow and green. Then everything went back to normal.

Aisha Mohammoud (10)
Somerville Primary School, Birmingham

The Mystery Man!

Whilst I was thrown into the dark, ebony cave, I finally saw a light in the distance. I zoomed across the cave but as I got closer the gleaming light disappeared. I turned around and saw a sharp knife, which glistened with the reflection of my face on it.

Suddenly ...

Nabila Irshad (10)
Somerville Primary School, Birmingham

Where Am I?

I walked in the weird, enigmatic mansion. I don't even know how I'd got there! I took one pace and there I saw a white ghostly figure, I looked upon its face …

It smiled an eerie smile at first, I didn't know what to do so I looked behind but no one was there, I turned back, then I knew why it had smiled at me.

Then it clasped on me, its hand was like cold, damp, wet soil and its nails were like a knife stabbing me in the heart. I suddenly heard something! It was a mouse scampering, all of this freaked me out.

I froze and fell to the ground and my lips wouldn't move! I tried to move but I couldn't, but why? Then finally I yelled, 'Argh!'

As I yelled, the figure I had seen disappeared. Then I ran like a cheetah catching its prey just in case it came back, but was it real or not? I never ever found out the answer and I didn't tell anybody either. would they have believed me?

Fozia Gul (10)
Somerville Primary School, Birmingham

The Dungeon

I saw a rat crawling as slowly as a tortoise. Closer and closer it came to me. I got even more scared. I slowly ran across the floor. I started to sweat more and more from my neck. *'I hate rats!'* I kept saying to myself. I opened my eyes, the rat had disappeared.

Madihah Hasan (8)
Somerville Primary School, Birmingham

The Castle Of Secrets And The Golden Key

Long ago, in a faraway land, there was a king called Arthur. Arthur had heard about a golden key. One day he ordered his servants to go and look for the golden key. He'd also heard that it opened the castle of secrets.

His servants looked for days, but whenever they came back they had nothing. King Arthur got fed up. One day he himself went to look for it.

He went deeper and deeper into the deep, damp woods. When King Arthur looked into an owl's nest ... *there it was,* just lying there as still as gold. He grabbed the box. It said: 'A kind king like Arthur deserves this. If King Arthur finds this, he can keep it'.

Amel Mohammed (8)
Somerville Primary School, Birmingham

The Haunted Castle

One day Stephan was walking. An hour later he was lost. He tried to find his way home, but he couldn't. Suddenly he saw a castle. He knocked on the door, then a weird man opened the door. He said, 'You can stay here for the night.' It was night, so Stephan went to bed.

Thunder struck while he was asleep. He was thirsty so he got himself some water. When he went back in the bed, the door opened and ... he felt something touching him, and that was the end of Stephan.

Jansheer Khan (8)
Somerville Primary School, Birmingham

Mini Saga

I was in the toilet when I heard a ghostly scream and I was scared out of my wits. Then ... my daddy came and reassured me that there was no ghosts or ghouls in our house.

I went back to my bedroom and went to sleep in my fluffy bed.

Danyal Hassan (9)
Somerville Primary School, Birmingham

Mini Saga

I was all alone downstairs. The stairs were making creaky noises. My hands were shaking. My head was spinning. It was like there was someone in the kitchen, I wanted to go upstairs but the door was locked then ... My mum came and put on the light.

Shahid Zaman (9)
Somerville Primary School, Birmingham

The Dragon

The green scaly dragon was lying in his dark, dank cave amongst his treasure. Suddenly he heard a scuffling noise in the distance. He saw a flickering light as the noise grew louder and louder. The light got steadier and he heard excited voices. *Yummy,* he thought, *tourists for supper!*

Jenny Yule (8)
The Croft Preparatory School, Stratford-upon-Avon

Swimming Pools

I jumped into the water, my hands clutching my knees, I hit the water, *splash*. I sunk to the bottom. I started to struggle frantically and then I tried to swim to the top but, suddenly, someone else jumped on top of me and I was pushed to the bottom again.

Savanaugh Robertson (8)
The Croft Preparatory School, Stratford-upon-Avon

Shark Attack

One day there was a boy called Jack. He went to Wales to go sailing in a big boat. After a while he saw a splash. He thought it was a dolphin so he jumped in. All he saw was razor-sharp teeth: it was a shark!

Henry Tribe (8)
The Croft Preparatory School, Stratford-upon-Avon

Hedgehog Rescue

We were going on a walk and I spotted a hedgehog at the side of the path. I thought he was ill because he was out in the day and he wasn't moving. I decided to call him Snuffles because he was always sniffing about. Dad went back into the house and got out some leather gloves. He put them on and picked Snuffles up and put him in a big shoebox. We poured some water into a dish and gave it to Snuffles who started to drink it.

We took him to the vets and a nice lady called Fay helped to put him in a big cage and gave him some spray to get rid of his ticks. We said goodbye and drove home. With all the excitement, I nearly forgot it was Father's Day!

Sadly Snuffles died overnight but if we had left him he wouldn't have stood a chance.

Molly Wright (8)
The Croft Preparatory School, Stratford-upon-Avon

Robbie's Aeroplane Adventure

One day a 14-year-old boy called Robbie and his mother, Dianna, were washing their clothes in their back garden, when they saw lots of army men marching behind their gate. One of them was Robbie's father wearing a pilot helmet with all kinds of greens. (Robbie's father flew the Vulcan bomber.)

'World War II has begun men!' shouted the sergeant in a big voice. 'Get into the van boys!'

'Yes, Sir!' they said. Then they drove off into the mist.

Four years later, Robbie was eighteen and joined the army as a pilot, like his father, but he flew a Gnat plane. Robbie really enjoyed being a pilot.

One day, as the weather was cloudy and damp, ten Spitfires and a big Vulcan bomber, were dropping bombs over the army base. Robbie and his father ran as fast as they could to their planes. Robbie raced his plane behind the Spitfires and his father went on top. The other half were waiting in London with a few biplanes, they were going to go when the Vulcan bomber was blown up, they could destroy the Spitfires without getting destroyed by the Vulcan bomber.

They eventually destroyed the Vulcan bomber. Then they destroyed the Spitfires but the Germans kept on going so America dropped a new kind of bomb on Japan, the Germans stopped.

Hugh Symons (8)
The Croft Preparatory School, Stratford-upon-Avon

A Pony Dream

My heart pounded and my fingers froze. Puffin was about to jump. I closed my eyes as he lifted his front legs. *Crash!* I woke up. I looked round. I had fallen out of bed, and there were cupboards not jumps. Luckily, I was not jumping in the Grand National this year!

Anastasia Hall (8)
The Croft Preparatory School, Stratford-upon-Avon

Three Girls And A Bunny

One day three girls were asked by their mum to go and cut some firewood. The three went to the wood and started cutting, soon after they were very tired and wanted to have a bit of fun before they went home so they went exploring in the woods. After hours and hours had gone, it was getting dark, the youngest of the three was getting frightened so the oldest tried to comfort her.

In the morning the girls found themselves not in the wood but down a hole with a rabbit. When the girls had all woken up, they slid out of bed and got down on their hands and knees and crawled around on the floor trying to find the kitchen. In the kitchen they found the Easter bunny.

'I told you he was real,' said the youngest of the girls.

The rabbit was running about shouting, 'Argh, I'm late for Easter!'

'Excuse me.'

The rabbit stopped shouting and turned round, 'Yes?' said the rabbit.

'Who are you?'

'Why I'm the Easter bunny.'

The oldest had heard what the rabbit had said and had an idea, 'Let's help the Easter Bunny to hide the Easter eggs!'

'What a great idea!' said the Easter bunny.

'Well let's get to it then!' said the youngest. When the job was done, the girls went back home.

Molly Hughes (8)
The Croft Preparatory School, Stratford-upon-Avon

Home Again

We knew it, we had it, after 40 years, and we trembled as the thought of it shook us. We went up the steps, the happiest people alive. The waiting was over. It was in our grip, we held it up high to the crowd.

We had won the World Cup!

Oliver Thomas (8)
The Croft Preparatory School, Stratford-upon-Avon

I Love Roller Coasters

We handed over the tickets and we got on. We did not know when it was starting. It went up and up until we got to the top, then suddenly we went down, sideways, up and upside down. Then it stopped and pulled us back in our seats.

I love roller coasters.

Harriet Edwards (8)
The Croft Preparatory School, Stratford-upon-Avon

The Bobcat's Hero

One fine sunny day a family of bobcats were dozing on the fresh green grass. They lived in an enchanted forest with beautiful butterflies but they longed to catch fish and bathe in the water, but a wicked monster guarded it.

One day the father was so smelly and so hungry that he really needed the river so he threw a nearby log, but it splashed the monster, 'Who dares jump into my river? I will tear you to pieces!' yelled the monster.

'I'm far too fat, you should wait for my wife, she's much more meatier than me,' Dad said sweetly.

So the next day Mum tried, she tried to leap in the river but the monster said, 'Who dares leap in my river, I will torture you for my tea!'

'I'm far too crunchy for you, you should wait for my baby, she is more tender and juicier than me,' she said politely.

A few days later the baby tried. 'Who dares pounce in my river? I will bash you and smash you and eat you for my supper!' growled the monster.

'Oh really,' she said casually. Then she dived for the monster's legs and started tickling him under the armpits and the monster fell with a huge *splash!* He fell down the waterfall and was never seen again. The bobcats could go in the water whenever they fancied.

Theresa Day (8) & Annie Bath (7)
St Joseph's RC Junior School, Nuneaton

Laurissa!

Melissa is a young girl who loves to discover new things. Her hair is as shiny as metal and as bronze as a medal. She has a sister called Laura who really annoys her, so much that Melissa always fights with her and throws stuff at her, like toys and flour. Melony is a young lady and Melissa's godmother - her teeth are as white as pearls.

Melissa was brushing her teeth when she heard someone knocking on the door. It was the postman with something for Melissa. She unwrapped the box to find it was from Melody. *Zap!* Melissa was sucked into the box. She zoomed out and told her sister. Laura said she didn't believe her so Melissa pulled and heaved Laura down the stairs and pushed her into the box. Melissa dived in after her. The next morning Laura and Melissa were making plans.

After a while they were out on the street raising money for the blind and deaf. They were going to build a town and call it 'Laurissa'. When they had finished collecting the money they rushed over to buy some bricks and roof tiles. They threw all the bricks into the box but they wouldn't go in, so they mailed Melony and her reply said they had to have one person inside and one person outside passing them in.

One year later the town was finally finished and it had trees as bright as the sun and the grass was as juicy as a lolly.

Elissa Johnston (8)
St Joseph's RC Junior School, Nuneaton

The Haunted House

One scary night in a faraway land a vampire with red nostrils and a green face was eating a dinosaur sandwich when he smelt a creepy-crawlie on his nose, he ate it.

24 hours later Jack and Ruby were exploring in the forest when they saw a house, a haunted house.

'Look,' shouted Jack.

'Let's explore that house,' wailed Ruby.

So both of them tiptoed into the house.

The vampire was very upset. 'I thought I'd killed them 15 years ago. Just wait until I punish them for this.'

The vampire disguised himself with his best costume. While Jack and Ruby were in the house the vampire arrived and quickly ate them.

They were always doomed.

Nadia Ahmed (8)
Somerville Primary School, Birmingham